SISTERS

Audrey P. Johnson

SCHOLASTIC INC.
New York Toronto London Auckland Sydney

Cover Photo by Owen Brown

ISBN 0-590-32183-8

Copyright © 1986 by Audrey Johnson. All rights reserved. Published by Scholastic Inc.

12 11 10 9 8 7 6 5 4 3 2   7 8 9/8 0/9

Printed in the U.S.A.   01

A Wishing Star Book

WISHING STAR TITLES
FROM SCHOLASTIC

CHAPTER
ONE

I wondered what my mother's reaction would be when she learned I was looking for a job. She was sure to say I should have waited until we were settled after our move from California to the Thousand Island region in upper New York State. There were still dishes to be unpacked and washed, boxes of clothing to be sorted and put away, places to be found for the books and collectibles that filled five large packing crates. Where would we ever find room for everything in my grandmother's house, which had two small closets and practically no cupboard space in the kitchen?

I drew the hood of my parka closer about my face and bent against the wind. The rain and snow had turned to sleet, and the little ice pellets stung my face as I walked along the shoulder of the road. I was sure I would never get used to this north country, with its ice and snow.

I was homesick for California where I could play tennis all day, soak up the sun beside a backyard swimming pool, or go hiking in the hills with Kevin. I wondered if I would ever see Kevin again.

The last six months had been a period of great change, and we were all still recovering.

My parents' divorce had not been a friendly, handshaking affair. There was a court battle with my parents fighting every step of the way. Our beautiful home had been sold and the money divided between my mother and father. The house was heavily mortgaged, and after all the bills were paid there wasn't much money left.

My grandmother had died during the winter and left her home in the resort region to my mother. After much deliberation, Mother decided we should move here. "The house is paid for," she had explained to my sister Rae, my brother Mac, and me. "Moving our furniture across the country will be a big expense, but once we're there we'll have only taxes and living expenses. I'm sure we can manage."

Mac, a second-year medical student in Atlanta, thought it was a good idea. But for Rae and me it was a grim experience to leave our friends and start in a new school in the middle of the year.

Many long-distance phone calls were made between my mother and Uncle Bob, who still lived in the area. He assured us the house was sound but needed work. "There's a barn on the property, and I'll have Grandma's furniture moved out there before you arrive. Later you can decide how much of it you want to keep. I'll also have someone come in and clean the house." Grandma had been in a nursing home for the two years before her death.

We arrived in March in the midst of a howling

blizzard, and the taxi had followed the snowplow all along the river road. Our furniture had not arrived. We learned later that the moving van was stranded on the Northway, sixty miles away. In our lightweight clothing we battled the snowdrifts all the way from the road. Mother and I were both trying to help Rae, who was having a hard time.

"It's March first," my mother complained, struggling through the drifts. "Who would have expected a blizzard this late?"

The house was a shock. I had visited there as a child, but I had forgotten how small the rooms were, how dark the woodwork and the wallpaper. The floors were uneven and they squeaked when we walked over them. The linoleum on the kitchen floor was worn, the sink pitted and stained. The house had the musty smell of very old houses. Remembering what we had left behind in California, it was hard to hold back the tears.

Uncle Bob had arranged to have the electricity turned on and the oil tank filled for the furnace. So we had lights and heat but nothing else. The storm continued, and as darkness fell I felt like we were marooned on a little island.

"Don't worry," my mother said. "The storm won't last forever. I'm sure the roads will be open tomorrow."

"We're all alone," I protested. "We don't have anything to eat."

"Uncle Bob will reach us as soon as the roads are cleared. We couldn't expect him to drive fifteen miles during a raging blizzard. Everything will look brighter in the morning. This is beautiful country, and the St. Lawrence River is only a few hundred feet from our back porch."

Big deal, I thought. Right now I would have traded the whole St. Lawrence Seaway for one of Mexican Sam's tacos back home.

"I have some candy bars in my flight bag," Rae offered.

My mother and I exchanged smiles. Rae was a candy freak, and we might have known she wouldn't travel three thousand miles without a supply of it. Rae sat on the floor rubbing her feet to warm them. She had worn sandals on the plane, and she put them on the radiator to dry. A birth defect had left Rae with a slight limp, the kind you might have if you had a blister on your foot, but it was enough to mark her as different. In elementary school I used to get into fist fights when the kids teased her about it. Now she was fifteen and a sophomore in high school. She was really beautiful, with tawny hair and sea-green eyes, but as she grew older she had withdrawn into a shell, overly conscious of her handicap.

I was the outgoing one from the time I could walk, and I was always getting into trouble. I got lost at family reunions, I tore my clothes playing football with the boys, I let a herd of cows loose when I visited my Uncle Frank's farm. When I was eleven I had published a one-time newsletter that had the neighborhood in an uproar because I printed some gossip my reporters had brought me.

Rae never caused any trouble. She never got dirty. She never got carsick or brought notes home from the teacher. Our relatives and the neighbors loved her. I loved her, too. All my life I had thrown a protective shield around her, trying to keep people from hurting her. I felt guilty that I was strong and healthy and popular.

My mother was standing by the window looking out at the storm. She looked so tired. The last few months had been hard on her. I hoped she wouldn't break down and cry because then I would, too. It seemed unreal being in this empty room on a cold March day, so far from everything that was important to us.

She turned to face us. "I'm sorry, girls. I didn't plan this very well. I should have had Uncle Bob stock some groceries for us. I just didn't dream the weather would be this bad."

"We're survivors," I replied. "We'll eat Rae's candy bars and my face will break out, but we'll make it through the night." It was a poor attempt at humor, but I was trying to mask the mixed feelings I had.

My father had been the take-charge person, making all the decisions, and he had always given us a sense of security. Now our lives were turned upside down, and we would have to make decisions on our own. He had remarried and moved to Chicago. I couldn't help feeling resentful. Couldn't my parents have tried harder or at least stayed together until Rae and I were through high school? Didn't they care at all about our feelings?

My mother tried to be cheerful. "At least we'll each have our own bedroom. Why don't you girls pick out the ones you want right now and plan where you'll put your furniture?"

"It's a choice between the biggest bedroom with

the broken windowpane that has a piece of cardboard nailed over it, the small room with the stained ceiling, or the room where the wallpaper is coming loose," I said. If I sounded nasty I couldn't help it. I was hungry and homesick, and I was sure Kevin would never write to me.

"The one with the broken window overlooks the river," my mother said, ignoring my sarcasm. "You can see the Canadian mainland."

"I'll take the one with the loose wallpaper," Rae offered. "I'll take it off and paint a mural of the freeway on the wall."

A heavy pounding on the front door ended our isolation. Cautiously my mother approached the door. "Who is it?"

"We're your neighbors, the Tabers, from down the road. Can we be of any help?"

My mother opened the door, and a man and a boy stood outside, their heavy clothing coated with snow. Even their eyebrows were frosted white. "Hello," said the man. "I'm Roy Taber, and this is my son Chris. We run the marina down the road. We thought you might be short of supplies in the storm." He looked around the empty room. "That's an understatement."

"If you want a second opinion, you've got it." My mother laughed in relief. We greeted them like lifelong friends. They had brought beef stew in a thermos jug, a loaf of homemade bread, and coffee.

"All this good food and we don't have any dishes or silverware," Rae complained.

"Chris, run home and get some utensils for these

ladies. We can't have them eating with their fingers," Mr. Taber said.

I judged Chris to be about sixteen. He was tall and blond, with the bluest eyes I had ever seen. I wondered if he would be in my junior class at school.

Rae had slipped her sandals back on and sat cross-legged on the floor. I noticed Chris was watching her and I didn't blame him; she was so pretty.

"One of you girls want to ride back on the snow-mobile with me?" he asked. He really addressed his question to Rae.

"We'd like to but we just have lightweight clothing with us," she answered.

"Give us a raincheck," I said. "The only snow-mobiles I've seen were on TV, and I always wanted to ride on one."

"It's our chief method of transportation in the bad storms we get up here. We've been called in on medical emergencies or to take food to families stranded when the roads are closed," Chris answered.

When Chris returned, he and his father went out to the barn where Grandma's things were stored. With the aid of a lantern they found some mattresses, which they carried back through the snow to the house. On their second trip they located an electric hot plate, a teakettle, and a wooden blanket chest in which some handmade quilts were stored.

They arranged the mattresses on the living room floor, and we covered them with quilts. "I guess you're all set for the night," Mr. Taber said. "We'll check back in the morning."

I walked to the door with Chris. "What year are you in school?" I asked.

"This is my junior year. School will probably be closed tomorrow. The plows won't be able to reach all the back roads. I drive to school, so I'll pick you and your sister up in my jeep when you're ready to register."

"We won't register until Monday. We have so much work to do here. Besides, we'll have to shop for some warm clothes before we can start school."

"The seasons change abruptly here," Mr. Taber said. "By next week it could be fifty degrees. The ice should be off the roads in a couple of weeks."

"You'll like the north country," Chris added. "It's a great place for winter sports, and in the summer everyone goes boating, fishing, and water skiing." He turned to Rae. "Do you water-ski?"

She shook her head. "No."

He smiled. "Then I'll teach you."

I knew what Rae was thinking. Chris didn't know about her limp yet. She was wondering if he would still be interested in her when he did notice. Or would he continue being nice to her because he felt sorry for her?

I wanted to shake her and tell her to meet life head-on, to put her handicap aside and make the most of her assets—her beauty, her artistic ability, her intelligence. But it wouldn't work. I had tried for years to build up her self-esteem. So my guilt trip continued.

"Well, at least we'll know one person in school when we register," I said to Rae after Chris and his father left. "I like him."

"He seems nice," she answered. She was on her hands and knees examining one of the handmade quilts. "Isn't it beautiful?" she said, running her hand over the pastel-colored blocks that formed circles on a white background. "But it's only half-finished."

"That's the wedding ring design," my mother answered. "Grandma must have been working on it when she was taken sick. I wonder if she meant it as a wedding gift for one of you girls?"

I looked closely at the tiny hand stitches, the hundreds of small blocks. Grandma must have been working on it for months. I could imagine her during the long winter evenings, bent over her sewing.

My mother smoothed down the blocks. "I'm sure Grandma planned one for each of you girls."

I wished I had known my grandmother better. I only remembered her from my childhood when we visited here, a small woman with white hair worn in braids wrapped around her head. When I was about six I went with her once to pick currants in the field in the back of the house. Later, we helped her make jelly by washing the jelly glasses brought up from the cool, dark cellar.

My grandfather had lived all his life along the river and had been a skipper for one of the tour-boat lines that traveled through the scenic Thousand Islands. He died four years before my grandmother, and she had chosen to stay on in her own home rather than come west to live with us.

It took me a long time to fall asleep that night. I thought about Kevin. He had promised to write, but I wondered if he would. We had planned to do so many things together this summer: learn to scuba dive, take bicycle trips through the state parks, volun-

camp for handicapped children. For ce, I touched his class ring, which I wore a gold chain around my neck. I wore it all the time, even to bed. We were so alike, Kevin and I, interested in so many things. Would he find someone else now that I was gone?

Maybe I could find a job and earn enough money for a plane ticket to fly back for a few weeks this summer and stay with my friend Sue. I didn't want Kevin or my friends back home to forget about me. A trip would give me something to look forward to and help me to cope with all the things that were happening.

I heard Rae sigh in her sleep. I knew she was worried about the adjustments of our new life and starting in a new school. It was challenging for me, too, but I hoped I could bluff my way through.

Not a cloud could be seen in the incredibly blue sky the next morning. The icicles on the eaves were melting, and the sun was so bright on the snow it hurt your eyes. Chris had plowed out the driveway at daybreak so the moving van could unload, and he told us that all the main roads were open.

The movers arrived around ten o'clock and soon the little house was overflowing with furniture, appliances, and packing crates. Our modern furniture looked strangely out of place. "I'm afraid some of the furniture will have to join Grandma's in the barn," my mother said. "We just haven't got room for everything."

I had my own bedroom, but my furniture looked alien against the dark wallpaper in the room I had chosen. I remembered my bright, airy bedroom over-looking the swimming pool back home. Without enthusiasm, I began to unpack my shorts, my bikinis, my tennis dresses.

Uncle Bob stopped by in the afternoon. He helped put up the beds and move some of the crates of furniture into the woodshed off the kitchen until we had time to unpack them. We learned we needed additional wiring before our electric stove could be hooked up, and we also needed extensive plumbing before we could use our washing machine.

"I'm going to need a car," my mother said. "We're absolutely stranded here three miles from town. Do you think you could find me a good used car?"

"I'll take you to one of the better used car dealers in town," Uncle Bob replied. "Do you have anything in mind?"

"The smallest, most economical model I can find," she answered. I remembered the sports car she had driven in California. Mom sighed. "We need paint —gallons of it—and wallpaper. A new sink is an absolute necessity, and I have to do something about floor covering in the kitchen. No matter how I scrub that worn linoleum, it doesn't look clean."

"Will the weekend be soon enough?" Uncle Bob asked.

"Of course. In the meantime, we're going to need groceries."

"Chris offered to take us shopping this afternoon," I said.

"Good. Then you girls can get some warm clothes for school, too. I'll make out the grocery list."

"Who is Chris?" Uncle Bob asked.

"Chris Taber. His father runs the marina nearby."

"You'll find the people here very friendly. They'll take time out to help you."

Uncle Bob left, promising to send an electrician and a plumber to hook up our appliances. "It's going to be a real challenge cooking on a hot plate," my mother said. We found coffee in one of the packing crates and dug out our coffeemaker and some cups. We took a break after we vacuumed the rugs and put linens on the beds.

Chris came stomping in out of the cold. "Is everybody ready for the trip to town?"

"The girls are going to ride into town with you," my mother answered. "Sit down and have some coffee first."

"You go, Robin," Rae said, stirring her coffee. "I want to get my room settled."

I was annoyed. Rae was carrying this too far. "You need clothes for school. You can't wear your sundresses."

"You can shop for me. We're both the same size and you know what I like."

"Come with us, Rae," Chris urged. "I'll show you the town. Not that it will take long."

She smiled at him. "Thanks just the same. There's plenty of time for me to see the town."

I knew it was useless to argue with Rae when she made up her mind. "What am I going to wear? I can wear a sweater under my jacket, but I haven't got any boots."

"I'll carry you to the jeep." Chris looked so big, so comfortably strong, I decided to let him. My mother made out the grocery list while I tried to find a warm sweater among my things.

When we left the house, Chris scooped me up in his arms. I hung on to him. "Don't let me fall!" I shrieked as he half-jogged, carrying me to the jeep.

"You'll only land in a snowdrift," he said, laughing. Settled in the jeep with the heater going full blast, we started down the road. It was a fairyland world with snow etching the tree branches against the blue sky.

"Why did you leave California?" Chris asked, his face serious.

"It's a long story."

"Rather not talk about it. Right?"

"Right." I wasn't ready to go into our personal life with Chris. Maybe someday, when I knew him better, I would tell him about my parents' divorce.

We drove along a few minutes in silence. Then Chris pointed down the river to a cluster of buildings and docks extending out into the ice. "That's our marina. There's nothing doing now, of course, but as soon as the ice breaks in the river it's busy until late November."

"Do you work with your father?"

He nodded. "I've grown up on the river. I plan to study marine biology in college. Do you have any other brothers and sisters besides Rae?"

"My brother Mac is a medical student."

"I'm impressed," Chris said.

I went on, "He's a superbrain and has won all kinds of scholarships. Rae is the artistic one and has won lots of awards. I'm the one with no special talents."

"I don't believe that. What are you interested in?"

"I've done volunteer work with youth groups. I'd like to get a degree in criminal justice and really be able to help young people in trouble."

"Heavy!" Chris exclaimed.

"Yes, I suppose it is, but that's what I'd like to do. I've worked with children who were disadvantaged and had emotional problems, and I can understand why some of them get into trouble."

We reached town and drove down Main Street. I counted only a few stores besides the post office and a diner. There was a hardware store, a sporting goods store with boat motors and fishing equipment in the window, a grocery store, and a small department store. Chris pulled up in front of the department store. "Barnard's carries a good line of clothes. You should be able to find something here."

The store was small and overcrowded with stock, but I noticed they carried national brand names. I bought a pair of corduroy jeans and a pair of dress jeans for both Rae and me, along with some velour tops. I was looking through some suede jackets on the rack when Chris said, "A ski jacket with a hood would be warmer and more practical for now. You'll want to dress warm for that snowmobile ride I promised you, and there's still time for some skiing."

I picked a light-blue-and-navy jacket for me and, at Chris's suggestion, a green one for Rae. "It'll match her eyes," he said.

"Very observant of you," I commented. "I didn't know you got that close to Rae."

"A girl's eyes are the first thing I notice." I knew I should be glad Chris was attracted to Rae, but I

14

couldn't help feeling a tiny stab of jealousy. Chris had a way of making a girl feel very special. I liked that about him.

Warm knit caps, gloves, and boots completed my shopping. The bill was astounding, but my mother had given me her credit card. As soon as I was working I would help pay for my clothes.

Our next stop was the grocery store, and judging from the list my mother had given me, I guessed she expected to be snowed in for the next three months. After we loaded the groceries in the car, we walked around the town. Many of the stores, like the souvenir shops, were closed for the winter and had little signs in the window: OPEN APRIL 15.

We ate pizza in a little restaurant down by the docks and watched the skaters on the river. "The river completely freezes over in the winter—you can walk across to Canada," Chris said. "Do you see that island out there with the towers of a castle showing?"

I nodded.

"That's Heart Island, where one of our famous landmarks was built, Boldt Castle. Have you heard the story about it?" Chris asked.

"No. It looks like a European castle you'd see in a travelogue."

"There's a very romantic story behind it. It was built as a valentine."

"Imagine getting a castle as a valentine! I'd like to go through it some time," I said.

"You can. It's a tourist attraction now. I'll take you and your sister there in my boat when the ice is gone."

It was growing dark as we drove home, and when Chris drove in the driveway he said, "It's nice to see lights in the house again. It's been dark for so long. I used to do errands for your grandmother—mow the lawn, trim the shrubbery, put up the storm windows. She baked the best molasses cookies in the neighborhood. I missed her when she was taken sick."

"Thanks for everything," I said as he helped me carry the groceries and the clothes into the house. "I hope everyone I meet here will be as nice as you, but I guess that's asking too much."

"Oh, I don't know about that," he smiled. "There are a lot of us good ol' boys around here."

Rae was seated at the kitchen table writing a letter as we came in. "I hope you like the clothes we picked out for you, Rae," Chris said as he put the bags down on the table.

"No problem," she replied. "Robin and I have the same taste in clothes. Not in much else, but in clothes."

"You have no excuse for staying in the house now. I'll pick you and Robin up tomorrow afternoon and take you both snowmobiling."

"Don't plan on me," Rae replied. She avoided his eyes.

"Why not?"

"I'm not the outdoor type." She tried to sound flippant.

Chris turned to me. "How about you, Robin? Are you the outdoor type?"

"Robin's the athletic member of the family," Rae offered.

"That's me. Strong muscles, weak mind," I replied.

Chris looked at Rae, then me, as if he was aware of an undercurrent he didn't quite understand. I felt embarrassed as I walked him to the door. "Thanks again. I'll see you tomorrow."

Back in the room, I turned to Rae after he left. "You didn't have to snub him like that. He likes you."

Rae answered with the quick temper of a guilty conscience. "Oh, sure he does! He hasn't seen me walk yet!"

"That's beside the point. Give the guy a chance!"

Rae threw down her pen. "That's easy for you to say! You don't even try to understand how I feel!" She went into her room and slammed the door.

"What was that all about?" my mother said, coming into the kitchen. She had been in the living room putting up curtain rods.

"Nothing much," I answered. I was confused over Rae's outburst. It wasn't like her to be ill-mannered or bitter. Perhaps she was overtired and upset by our moving, or maybe she really liked Chris and was apprehensive about how he would react when he saw her limp.

I started putting the groceries away. I had had such a good time with Chris and now it was all spoiled. The guilty feelings were crowding back again.

CHAPTER TWO

The next day we washed windows and the wood-work and put shelf paper in the kitchen cupboards. I helped Rae unpack her art supplies and some of her paintings and sketches.

"I can't wait to get this ugly wallpaper off so I can do something with this room," she said.

"Still going to do a mural of the freeway?"

"I was only kidding, of course. Maybe I'll do a nature scene, something to blend with the natural features of the land."

"Think snow," I commented.

"There's really no place for me to work in the house. I saw a little shed out back. Do you think I could fix it up as a studio?"

"If you mean the little shed with all the windows, I think it's a chicken house."

"Oh, no! Do you think we could clean it up? I'm serious. It would be a neat place for a studio, over-looking the river and the islands."

"We'll check it out when the snow goes. If it's worth fixing up, I'll help you."

18

After lunch, a Mrs. Creel, who represented the Welcome Wagon, called on us. She had all kinds of freebies for us—a haircut and blow-dry at the Modern Beauty Shoppe, dinner for two at the Maplewood Diner, a coupon for two loads of wash at the Laundromat, a half-gallon of ice cream from the Apple Tree Dairy.

"You're just going to love it here," Mrs. Creel said, smiling benevolently at all of us. She had a run in her stocking, and I was sure I had seen a hat like hers in a thirties late-night movie.

"It's like stepping back in time," my mother said. She was holding a plastic measuring cup and a bag of sponges Mrs. Creel had given her. "I grew up here and I don't think the town has changed one bit."

"Oh, but it has," Mrs. Creel replied, handing her a brochure of community activities. "We have off-track betting now and a new drive-in theater."

"You don't say!"

Mrs. Creel turned to Rae and me. "You girls may find it rather quiet here. I've heard about the wild lifestyles in California." She lowered her voice. "Is it really true what I read in the *Enquirer*?"

"It's even worse," I said with a straight face, noting Rae had turned away to keep from laughing. Shaking her head sadly, Mrs. Creel gathered up her papers and put them in her embroidered tote bag.

After she had gone, my mother looked through the complimentary copy of the town's weekly newspaper. "I'm going to have to get a job." She read aloud from the Help Wanted column: " 'Registered nurse for Sunnyside Nursing Home.' That's out. 'Demonstrator for jewelry parties.' No way! I've seen the

19

jewelry. 'School-bus driver.' Now that's a possibility!"

Rae and I burst out laughing. My mother's driving was a family joke. Rae said, "Remember the time you backed into a state trooper's car?"

"I didn't have my mind on my driving at the time."

"You took your driver's test three times before you passed," I reminded her.

Rae added, "Would you really jeopardize the lives of those innocent little schoolchildren?"

"I'm serious," my mother said. "I'm going to look into the job. I was a secretary before I married your father, but the thought of working in an office with young girls just out of high school or business school terrifies me. I'd feel like their den mother. With my rusty skills I'd be a disaster—I could never cope with the new business machines."

"No thanks. A school-bus driver job seems like a good idea. I'd be home when you girls have time off from school."

"We're not little kids anymore, Mom. We can stay alone," I reminded her.

She looked hurt. "In other words, you don't need me?"

"I didn't mean that, Mom."

Her voice had a worried, twisted sound. "I'm sure the business world doesn't need another displaced homemaker, either." She got up and started clearing off the table.

What's wrong with all of us? I thought. We're so quick to take offense these days. Is it the transition we're going through? My mother had surprised me since my father left. She'd never worked outside our home since she was married. Suddenly she was on her own, but she had shown a resilience and determination I hadn't believed her capable of.

During the divorce proceedings she had asked little for herself, but she had insisted that my father provide a trust fund so Mac could finish medical school and Rae and I could go to college. Now, at forty-two, she had to enter the work force again and it was going to be difficult for her.

Later, I looked through the want ads myself. I saw an ad for part-time work at Neuman Florist on Saturdays. When I had ridden into town with Chris, I had noticed a row of greenhouses about a half-mile down the road from our house. I wondered if that was the place. If so, I could easily walk to work. I decided to look into the job.

Wearing my new jeans and ski jacket, I went outside around three o'clock to wait for Chris. The yellow school buses had been lumbering past the house, and I knew Chris would be driving home from school.

I dug the snow away from the mailbox by the road and I wondered when I would be hearing from my friends. Penny, Sue, and Jennifer had promised to write, and of course Kevin. Strange, I hadn't thought about Kevin today. I had been thinking of Chris and going snowmobiling this afternoon.

I experimented making snowballs and rolled one along the ground, watching it become bigger and bigger. I wondered if I had time to make a snowman. Then I heard a motor in the distance, and shading my eyes against the glare from the sun, I could see a blue-and-orange snowmobile racing across the fields toward the house. It was Chris. I recognized his white ski cap and red jacket. I felt a glow of happiness, knowing I would be spending the next few hours with him.

What was wrong with me? A few days ago I had cried because I was leaving Kevin and now I was looking forward to being with this new boy I had just met. I just knew that Chris made me feel very special and I liked being with him.

He crossed the road and came into our driveway. "Hi!" he called, shouting to make himself heard above the noise of the snowmobile. "Ready?" His face was ruddy from the cold, and strands of blond hair straggled from under his cap. "Climb in the back and hold on. I'm going to take you out on the river."

"No! We might go through the ice!"

"Trust me. The ice is still strong. Sunday they were driving cars on the river." As the machine leaped forward, the wind carried my protests away. We flew across the fields and began a gradual descent to the river.

The islands extended as far as I could see, rising through the ice. Some were so small they contained only a few pine trees. Many of the larger islands were the site of spacious summer homes. As we sped across the ice, Chris shouted out the names of some of the islands: Devil's Oven, Grindstone Island, Rock Island (with its lighthouse), the Lost Channel.

I relaxed when I saw the ice wasn't going to crack

and we weren't in any danger. I tried to visualize how the islands would look in the summer, green and inviting and inhabited by vacationers.

We passed other snowmobiles and an occasional iceboat skimming across the ice with sails unfurled. What a different world, I thought as I clung to Chris. Will I ever fit into it?

In the distance I could see a giant bridge hop-scotching the islands. As we drew near, Chris turned the snowmobile toward the shore under one of the girders of the bridge. He shut off the motor and the sudden quiet was eerie. The only sound was the hum of traffic far overhead on the bridge.

"This is the international bridge that joins Canada and the United States," Chris said. "How did you like your ride?"

"Great, after I decided I wouldn't end up on the bottom of the river with the snowmobile."

"I'll let you drive the snowmobile back."

"No way! I'm still afraid of all this ice and snow."

"Get out and stretch your legs." He helped me up, then bent down and brought out a thermos from a kit on the snowmobile. "I brought some hot choco-late. I thought you might be cold."

He took off his gloves and poured the steaming chocolate into styrofoam cups, and we sat down on a snowy ledge to drink it. I took off my gloves and curled my fingers around the cup to warm them. Our eyes met and we smiled at each other. I felt so at ease with Chris. I didn't have to be witty or clever or entertaining. I could just be myself—I had never felt this way with a boy before.

Chris picked up a broken branch and made designs in the snow. "Your sister's not very friendly, is she?"

"She's just shy," I answered. What could I say? I wasn't going to tell him the real reason.

"I have the feeling she doesn't like me."

"Why shouldn't she like you?" It hurt to remind myself that Chris had been attracted to Rae the very first day.

He tossed the branch aside. "It doesn't matter."

I had the uncomfortable feeling it did matter to him. "Give her time. It takes a while for her to make friends." I wanted to change the subject. I didn't want to talk about Rae. "I'm looking for a job. I saw one advertised at Neuman Florist. Is it a good place to work?"

"The work is seasonal. I guess Mr. Neuman is all right. I never heard any complaints about him."

"I'll put my application in. I saw some greenhouses not far from our house, over there." I pointed to them. "Is that the place?"

"Right. Have you ever worked before?"

"Just volunteer work."

"Working in a greenhouse isn't easy," he warned me.

"Volunteer work isn't always easy, either. I've washed a lot of dishes for free."

We drank the rest of our hot chocolate, and then we hiked along the river. Coming back we had a snowball fight, but Chris was careful not to throw too hard. "I've got two sisters and I know what crybabies girls are." He laughed.

I retaliated by aiming a handful of snow at the

back of his head when he bent over to scoop some snow out of his boot. He turned his head and caught the snow full in his face. I gave a yell and he started to chase me. I fell in the snow and he landed beside me, pinning down my arms. "I ought to wash your face with snow," he threatened. His face was so close to mine, I noticed how blue his eyes were, with their thick lashes. For one crazy moment I thought he was going to kiss me, and I could hear the wild thumping of my heart. But he didn't kiss me; he threw me in a snow bank instead.

Our ride home was uneventful except for a spectacular apricot-and-gold sunset that looked like a celebration. The wind had frost on its breath and it tore at my lungs. I clung to Chris and buried my face against the back of his jacket. In March it grows dark early, and after the sun had set darkness gathered around us.

When we reached home Chris said, "While I'm here, I'll measure the broken window in that one bedroom—I promised your mother I'd repair it. We've got some old windows and I can cut the glass from one of them."

Rae was seated by the window writing a letter when we came in, tracking snow on the floor. Her shining hair fell across her shoulders like an advertisement for shampoo, and I found myself wishing for the thousandth time that I, too, had inherited the blond good looks of my father's side of the family.

"Where's Mom?" I asked her.

"She just washed her hair and she's blow-drying it."

"Mom," I called, "Chris is going to measure the glass for the window."

My mother came out of her bedroom. "Where's the tape measure? I have no idea where to look for it."

"It's in the box with the sewing machine accessories," Rae answered.

"Will you get it, dear?"

I saw the dismay in Rae's eyes. She couldn't hide her limp from Chris any longer. "I'll get it," I said quickly. Didn't I always try to protect her?

"No!" Rae's voice was almost a command. "I'll get it!" She got up from the table and walked across the room. To my astonishment, she seemed to be exaggerating her limp.

"What's wrong, Rae?" Chris asked. "Did you hurt yourself? I told you to leave the heavy stuff for me to move."

A frozen silence filled the room. Rae looked at him defiantly. "No, I didn't hurt myself. This is the way I am. You might as well know."

"I'm sorry," Chris stammered. "I didn't know."

"You don't have to be sorry. I was born a cripple and I'm used to it by now."

"Rae!" I was shocked. She had never used that word to describe herself before.

"Don't be so hard on yourself, Rae," Chris said quietly.

"Why shouldn't I be? Do you still want to teach me to water-ski?"

"Of course I do."

"It could be your good deed for the day. Teach

the handicapped to water-ski," Rae said spitefully.

I was too stunned to speak. This was Rae—my shy, quiet little sister. What feelings had been building up inside her to make her lash out at Chris this way?

He seemed to be studying her. "If you want me to feel sorry for you, forget it. I won't buy it."

Her face was unreadable. "I'm not interested in what you think."

"My best friend graduated from high school last year, and he was one of the most popular guys in school. He was in a wheelchair, but he was such a great guy the wheelchair didn't make any difference to us."

"Good for him!" I knew Rae was close to tears.

"So you can't really expect me to feel sorry for you, can you? Now, where's that yardstick?" Chris demanded.

Rae came back with the tape measure and threw it at him. He picked it up and went to measure the window. Rae went into her room and closed the door.

Disapproval was written all over my mother's face when Chris came back in the room. He was the first to speak. "I'm sorry if I was outspoken, Mrs. Thomas, but that's the way I feel. Rae has too much going for her to pull that act."

"I don't think it was necessary to speak so harshly to her."

"I have this bad habit of always saying what I think," Chris replied.

"Maybe we *are* too protective of Rae, Mother," I offered.

My mother turned her attention to me. "How can you say that? Have you ever had to cope with a handicap?"

I felt a sudden sadness. "Haven't I heard that all my life?"

Chris looked uncomfortable. "I'd better be going. My folks will be expecting me for supper. I'll cut the glass and put it in for you tomorrow. Good night, Mrs. Thomas. Good night, Robin."

He was gone and I was left facing my mother. She brushed past me and gave a light tap on Rae's door. Then she stepped inside and closed the door firmly.

I stood in the kitchen feeling a smoldering resentment. My mother and Rae had driven Chris away and he'd never want to come here again. It was bad enough to have to leave my friends and move here to live in this tacky house and start a new life for myself in a strange school. If I was four years old I would have thrown a tantrum. That's what I felt like doing now—screaming my frustration at Rae and my mother. I would have yelled about my father, too, for not trying harder to keep our family intact.

I ran to the front door and opened it. I could see the snowmobile heading across the fields, its lights feeling the way through the darkness. I closed the door and stepped out into the night. I couldn't go back in the house. I had no one to talk to. I headed down the road in the opposite direction, walking rapidly and hoping I could walk away the anger that was churning inside of me.

The night was clear and cold and the stars swept across the whole arch of the sky. I walked by starlight for several miles and when I finally turned back I realized how tired I was. By the time I came to the curve in the road that brought our house into view, I felt calmer and most of my anger was gone. In its place was a feeling of loneliness.

When I let myself into the house, my mother and Rae were watching TV in the living room. "There's stew on the electric plate," my mother called out to me. "Heat it up for yourself."

I wasn't hungry. I went into my room, undressed, and fell asleep listening to tapes Kevin and I had made earlier that winter of our favorite music groups.

CHAPTER
THREE

The next day was Saturday, and no one mentioned the blow-up of the night before. It was as if it had never happened, but I knew it lay just below the surface of our thoughts. Until last night, no one had ever dared to challenge Rae.

Uncle Bob arrived around ten o'clock to take my mother into town to look for a used car. Rae had decided to go along to see if she could find material for a skirt. I volunteered to stay home and wait for the electrician who was coming to install the wiring for our electric stove. The telephone company had also promised to send a man to hook up the phone.

By noon the stove was ready to use, and I went on a cooking binge. I made a big kettle of chili, a batch of granola cookies, and some corn bread. Still, the time passed slowly. After the phone was installed I had an urge to call someone. But who could I call? Chris was the only person I knew around here and I wasn't sure how he felt about us now.

I decided to take a chance. I looked up his number in the new phone book and dialed. A child answered.

"Is Chris there?" I asked. "This is Robin Thomas calling."

"He's outdoors. I'll call him."

After a few minutes he was on the phone. "Sorry to take so long, Robin. I was working on my jeep." He sounded out of breath.

"I picked a bad time to call," I said.

"That's all right. I was just cleaning off the battery cables."

"Our phone was installed this morning. I wanted to give you our number."

"Good, I'll write it down," Chris said.

There was a pause after he wrote down the number. I knew last night deserved a comment but I didn't know how to go about it. Instead I said, "Would you like to come over this evening and listen to records? You might want to tape some of them."

"Sorry, I don't think I can make it tonight. I came on too strong last night—I'm not sure how your mother will feel about my coming."

"My mother says what she thinks. You always know where you stand with her but she doesn't hold a grudge," I offered.

"I'm the same way. Then we should get along great."

"My mother hasn't forgotten all you did for us. Of course you're welcome here," I assured him.

"Just the same, I'd better cool it for a while. My big mouth is always getting me in trouble."

"Are you still planning on taking us to school Monday?"

"I'm planning on it. I'll be there about seven-fifteen," he said.

There wasn't much more to say. I said good-bye and hung up. A long Saturday afternoon stretched ahead of me with nothing to do but watch TV or read. Sunday loomed ahead, even more boring. It could have been a great weekend with Chris, but my mother and Rae had spoiled it.

By two o'clock they hadn't come home, and I was so bored I was nearly out of my mind. I remembered the job advertisement in the local paper. Saturday afternoon was probably a poor time to apply for a job, but I had to do something on my own. I felt as if I had been bounced around like a volleyball, with everyone else shaping my life. It was time to take definite action and make plans of my own.

Outside, snow mixed with rain was sweeping across the road. I pulled the hood of my ski jacket close around my face and bent against the wind. The Saturday afternoon traffic was heavy, so I kept to the shoulder of the road, sidestepping the puddles of water edged in ice. I was nearly frozen when I reached a big white house set back from the road. Behind the house were the greenhouses and a red-and-white sign announced, P.J. NEUMAN, WHOLESALE FLORIST. A pale blue delivery van was parked outside.

Nervously I clutched my scrap of newspaper clipping. I had never applied for a job before and I wondered how I should act. Should I act self-assured and aggressive or just plain humble? I turned down the long driveway, and when I came to the first greenhouse I hesitated. The structures were numbered one through eight. I took a chance and opened the door of the Number 1 greenhouse.

Stepping inside was like moving the calendar ahead into the lush, flower-scented days of spring. I felt the warm air and smelled the rich, moist earth. Row after row of tightly budded Easter lilies and pots of tulips and hyacinths, arranged on plant benches, filled one side of the long greenhouse.

At the end of the row a boy with a hose was watering the plants, sending a fine spray over flats of marigolds and petunia seedlings. I made my way carefully down the narrow aisle over the wet earth floor. The boy saw me and shut off the hose. "Hi, can I help you?" He was dark-haired and tall with a muscular build.

"I'm Robin Thomas and I'm answering your ad in the paper for help."

"My father is making a long-distance telephone call but he should be back shortly, if you don't mind waiting," he answered.

"I'll wait. I guess the job isn't filled yet."

"No, we'll be hiring at least three more people. Our busy season is just starting. Have you worked around plants before?"

"I've helped my mother with her plants," I told him.

He hesitated. "Taking care of a few African violets or spider plants is a lot different from working here. We raise tens of thousands of flower and vegetable plants, as well as decorative plants for homes and public buildings." He seemed to be discouraging me.

"I expected that. I'm willing to learn." Did he have to act so superior?

"I didn't mean to put you down. I just wanted to

point out that the work is hard. We have trucks to load for market, deliveries to make, trays of plants to be transferred from one greenhouse to the other. And later in the season the temperature gets up to over a hundred degrees in here."

"I'm not afraid of work and I'm used to hot temperatures. I'm from California."

He crossed his arms and leaned back against a post. "To be honest, Robin, we had boys in mind for the jobs," he said.

"The work doesn't sound like anything I'd have trouble with."

He frowned. "I haven't seen you at school. How long have you lived around here?"

"We just moved here a few days ago," I answered.

"Well, maybe we do things a little slower around here. We feel there are jobs for men and jobs for women."

"Oh, come on! We're in the eighties. Remember? Don't be so macho!" I'm doing everything wrong, I thought. This is no way to apply for a job, but his attitude annoyed me.

He flushed. "It's up to my father, of course. He's coming now." A middle-aged man in white coveralls was coming down the aisle. "Dad, this is Robin Thomas and she's applying for work."

Mr. Neuman smiled. "Hello, Robin. Come in my office and we'll talk about the job requirements."

I followed him down the aisle into a small office and sat down opposite him. "Do you have a driver's license?" He asked. "We need someone who can make deliveries."

"Yes, I took driver's training last fall and got my license."

"The job pays three-fifty an hour. We're looking for someone who can work all day Saturday and occasionally after school when we're extra busy around the holidays," he explained.

"I can work those hours," I agreed.

"Would transportation be a problem?"

"No, I live up the road about a quarter of a mile."

"You must be the family who moved into the Van Alystyne house."

"It was my grandmother's house," I told him.

"I'm glad to see someone has moved into the house. It's been vacant so long."

I sighed. "Please, don't remind me. We have so much fixing up to do."

"If your father is handy, he can probably do a great deal of the work himself."

I looked down at my hands. I hated explaining my family situation. "There's just my mother, my sister, and me. My brother's away at college."

"I see." Mr. Neuman shuffled the papers on his desk. Was he going to turn me down?

"Your son said you were looking for a boy for the job. I'd like to show you I could do the work," I offered.

He regarded me thoughtfully. "Jeffrey did suggest a boy for this particular job. We've already hired women to do the transplanting."

So that was his name. Jeffrey. He was an arrogant idiot! I sat there quietly. The interview would probably end with Mr. Neuman telling me he'd call in a few days and let me know his decision. By then he probably would have hired a muscle-bound football player. I stared at the brightly colored advertisements for seeds on the walls—petunias in every color from flaming red to deep purple, hybrid zinnias in deep yellow and salmon pink, feathery white asters.

I wanted this job. I wanted to dig in the moist earth and work with flowers that reminded me of my native California. I could try to forget this frozen north country that was so foreign to me.

Mr. Neuman leaned back in his chair. "Could you start work next Saturday, Robin?"

"You bet!" I exclaimed. I had the job! My first paying job!

"Fine. We'll expect you at eight o'clock Saturday." He went to the door and called, "Jeffrey, could you come here a moment, please?"

I supressed a smile. I wondered how Jeffrey was going to like this. He looked at me suspiciously when he came into the office.

"Robin will be joining our work crew on Saturday," Mr. Neuman said. "We won't expect her to do any heavy lifting, but I think she is capable of handling the rest of the work."

Jeffrey merely scowled at me. Mr. Neuman continued, "She can start by preparing the flats for the salvia and zinnia plants in the Number 4 house."

"Boys have always handled that job." Jeffrey turned to me. "I hope you won't quit the first time you break a fingernail."

"If you knew me better you wouldn't say that." I

smiled at Mr. Neuman. "Thank you for hiring me. I'll be here Saturday."

"You'll need boots, Robin. The earth floors in the greenhouses are muddy and slippery from the constant watering we have to do. Bring a pair of gloves, too. Handling the wooden flats can make your hands rough."

I said good-bye without glancing at Jeffrey. I hoped I looked businesslike as I left the office and started briskly down the aisle. Mr. Neuman's warning about the slippery floors was forgotten, and when I reached the Easter lilies, both feet shot out from under me and I plopped down suddenly on the wet floor.

I looked around quickly to see if Jeffrey had been watching; he was. He hurried toward me and helped me up. "Are you all right?"

I could have died with embarrassment. "Yes, I'm fine." Only my pride was hurt.

"These floors are dangerous—you have to watch where you're walking. You could have hurt yourself." He was being superior again.

"I'll get used to them. I'm really all right." The seat of my pants felt damp. I tried to straighten myself up as I made my way toward the door. Score one for Jeffrey, but this was only the beginning. I had the job and that was what counted. Mr. Neuman wouldn't be sorry he hired me, and I'd show that arrogant Jeffrey how efficient a girl could be.

As I walked up the driveway toward our house, my mother was looking out the window. She flung open the door. "Robin Thomas, where have you been? I've been worried sick. You could have left a note!"

"Sorry you worried about me. I went job hunting."

"Job hunting! With all the work we have to do around here! We're not even settled yet!"

"I can hold a job and help you, too. I don't start work until next Saturday, and we can get a lot done around here by then. I'll be working just down the road at Neuman Florist."

"I'm not sure I like the idea. You have a new school to adjust to and working had better not interfere with your studies. We may be low on money, but we're not so desperate that you have to get a job right away. Why don't you wait until summer vacation?"

"I want to work, Mom, and earn my own money. It's just a Saturday job, but I may be called in occasionally to work afternoons," I argued.

"You'll have to give it up at the first sign it's jeopardizing your studies."

"Don't worry, Mom. I can get it all together. Since when did I study on Saturdays?" I put my jacket in the hall closet. "Did you find a car?"

"Don't change the subject. I meant what I said about your schoolwork. Yes, I found a small second-hand car. Your Uncle Bob said it was a good buy and economical to operate. I'm picking it up Monday."

"Good, we're mobile again," I said.

"I bought paint for the kitchen and the woodwork. The salesman let me bring home some wallpaper sample books—you girls can pick out the paper

38

for your bedrooms." She opened one of the sample books.

Rae looked up from the book she was reading. "I hate wallpaper. I'm going to paint my room."

"You can be as creative as you want to, Rae, as long as it's in your own room. I've suffered through too many of your creative decorating nightmares." My mother spoke emphatically.

"Those were all phases I was going through. I've matured since then," Rae answered.

"We hadn't noticed," my mother observed. "Have you matured enough to help get supper?"

On Sunday, we painted the kitchen a sunny yellow and the cupboards white, but the effect was spoiled by the tacky linoleum and the grey pitted sink. I remembered our butcher block countertops back home, the Tiffany lamp that cast a soft glow over the dining area, and the patio doors that looked out over the swimming pool.

My mother was so cheerful it was pathetic. Maybe she felt guilty about the divorce and about bringing us to this clunker of a house. If she was trying to make us believe fixing up this house was fun and games, she failed. I put the paintbrushes to soak in a bucket of water and gathered up the newspapers we had put on the floor. I don't know why we tried to protect the ugly linoleum from paint spatters.

My mother stood back and surveyed our efforts. "Country-style living is in now, girls. I've seen some beautiful illustrations of rooms in home decorating magazines."

"Sure, Mom," I said. "We're the homespun type."

She went on, "We could store some of our furniture and bring in some of Grandma's things from the barn for real country decor."

"Let's keep the stereo and the television." I was being nasty again.

She looked hurt. "I'm proud we're being self-reliant and independent. There's a satisfaction in turning adversity into advantage."

"What advantage? I hadn't noticed any," I said.

"I've heard you sound off in the past about rampant materialism," she replied. "Perhaps a new awareness will grow from all this." Our eyes met, and I was the first one to turn away. I felt ashamed. I wanted to be supportive, but I felt so mixed-up and unhappy. Everything was going wrong.

My brother Mac called that evening and I answered the phone. "Robin!" he said. "How are things going?"

"Hi, doc. Have you performed any brain surgery yet?" I joked.

"I'm scheduling a lobotomy for you next week. I need the practice."

"Very funny, weirdo." I was really proud of my brother but I couldn't let him know.

"Are you getting settled?" Mac seemed concerned.

"Yes, no thanks to you." I was joking, but I really missed him.

"You know I couldn't get time off this week. I'm taking exams now but I'm flying out next weekend."

"What for? To go skiing?"

"No, to help. Save the heavy jobs for me," Mac said.

"How would you like to insulate my bedroom, clean the furnace, and put a new ceiling in the bathroom?"

"Hold on! I've only got the weekend. How's Mom doing?"

"I'll let you talk to her. She's hovering over me." I passed the phone to my mother. I'd be so glad to see Mac. I needed to talk to him. He had a way of putting things in the right perspective.

I washed my hair and did my nails to get ready for school the next day. I told myself I wasn't trying to impress anyone as I laid out my new corduroy jeans and a velour top. Back home I would have known exactly what to wear, but here, in this frozen wasteland, the kids could dress like Eskimos for all I knew. And my hair. Why hadn't I thought to get it styled before we moved?

I was glad Chris was driving us to school tomorrow. At least Rae and I wouldn't have to walk into school alone. The new school would be especially hard for Rae; she didn't make friends easily. Back home she had one best friend, Theresa Daly, a girl as quiet and shy as Rae. Together they formed a little, self-sufficient island with their mutual interest in art. All through high school Rae had never had a date with a boy. She pretended she wasn't interested in boys.

The divorce had been difficult for her to understand or cope with. My father was a commercial artist, so Rae's talent formed a bond between them. At times I felt like an outsider when they discussed art or went to art shows together. They often spent

Saturdays or Sundays sketching at the lake or in the country.

I was looking for a pair of knee socks to wear the next day when Rae came into my room with a towel wrapped around her head. "Is the curling iron around here, Robin? I'm going to need it in the morning."

"It's in the top drawer of my dresser," I told her.

She sat down on the edge of my bed. "You've been quiet today. You're mad at me, aren't you?"

"You did act pre-adolescent last night," I admitted.

"I didn't mean to cause trouble between you and Chris, but he had no right to speak to me that way," Rae said angrily.

"He did have a point, you know."

"I wouldn't want my own brother to talk to me like that, let alone a stranger. How does he know how I feel?" she complained.

"He's really a nice person, Rae, and he likes you. He picked that green jacket for you. He said it matched your eyes."

She looked indignant. "What! He has a lot of nerve picking out my clothes! Let me wear your parka!"

"Oh, no. I picked the blue one for myself. That's what you get for not going shopping with us."

That ended the argument. Rae left my room and slammed the door after her.

CHAPTER FOUR

"I do not intend to ride to school with Chris Taber," Rae announced to my mother the next morning. "It's a case of mutual dislike. I don't know why you didn't bring the car home on Saturday. You could have driven us to school."

"My car won't be ready until noon today. With the price of gas, don't expect me to chauffeur you to school. It's not in my budget," Mother answered sharply.

"Then I'll take the bus."

"You'll do no such thing!" my mother answered emphatically. "You don't know the bus schedule and I won't have you standing around in the cold waiting for it. I don't want to hear another thing about it. Robin, what time did Chris say he'd pick you up?"

"Around seven-fifteen."

"It's nearly time then. You'd better get ready."

I took my parka out of the closet and handed Rae her green one. She gave me a pained look but she put it on. She scooped up her bright hair and arranged it about her shoulders.

"What a lovely color for you, Rae," Mother said.

Rae made a face. "I would never have picked out this color myself."

When Chris drove into the driveway and beeped his horn, Rae reluctantly followed me out to the jeep. Chris opened the door and I slid in beside him. Rae pulled herself in after me.

"Hi, Chris," I greeted him.

"Hi," he answered. Rae didn't speak. She stared straight ahead.

Chris leaned across me. "Hello, Rae." She turned her face away. He backed out of the driveway and started down the road. "Look, Rae, I didn't mean to hurt your feelings the other night."

She sat rigid and unforgiving. "I considered where it came from."

"In case you don't realize it, I'm trying to apologize."

"Don't bother!" The edges of her voice curled with scorn.

"Are you always so disagreeable in the morning?" Chris tried to make a joke of it.

"Only when I have reason to be. Why don't you just keep quiet and drive?" Rae said nastily.

I was becoming uncomfortable sitting in the middle with Chris and Rae jabbing verbal pitchforks at each other. "All right, you two! It's too early in the morning to listen to arguing. Chris, how about briefing us about the teachers?"

"Do you want the good news or the bad news?" he asked.

"Give me the bad news first," I answered.

"Well, there's Mr. Colburn, who teaches science. He hates every one under twenty-one."

"But that includes the whole student body."

"You got it. Miss Duncan, the girls' phys ed teacher, almost made the Olympic swim team but then she became allergic to chlorine. It made her neurotic, and we only hope she doesn't throw a piranha in the pool."

I was laughing, but Rae said disdainfully, "You're making it all up!"

"Wait—I haven't told you about Miss Van Zante, the music teacher. She's a frustrated songwriter whose songs never made the top ten. In fact, they never made the top eight hundred."

Rae wasn't amused. "They can't all be that weird. Does the school have a good art department?"

"I wouldn't know, but I do know the classes spend a lot of time down at the harbor sketching the lighthouse."

"Your making that up, too." Rae continued to be disagreeable.

"Everyone knows artists like to sketch lighthouses." Chris was grinning. "Did you ever see an artist without a sketch of a lighthouse?"

"You're not funny. In fact, you're obnoxious!"

I was glad when the high school came into view, but I felt some of my self-confidence ooze out of me when I saw the tide of students streaming toward the school. I'd be swallowed up in that mass of strangers. I prided myself on being cool, but it was disturbing just the same.

* * *

45

Chris gave us a brief tour of the school—our homeroom, the gym, the cafeteria, and the swimming pool. Then he took us to the office and introduced us to Mr. Tripp, vice-principal. Mr. Tripp was young and pleasant, and he had a curly beard that circled half his face. After he examined our school records and we filled out some forms, he called to his secretary, "Miss King, would you please ask Cory Siebert and Mariann Reynolds to come to the office?"

Cory looked like a Dallas cheerleader and seemed just as self-confident. Mariann was small and dark, with a ready smile. Mr. Tripp said, "Girls, we have two new students, Robin and Rae Thomas. Cory, since Robin's schedule is similar to yours, would you take her to classes today? Mariann, I'd like you to do the same for Rae. Rae has an impressive record in art from her former schools, so you two should have a great deal in common." He turned to Rae. "Mariann does the artwork for the school paper."

Out in the hall, Cory turned to me. "There's only ten minutes left of English class, so we might as well talk." We walked down the hall, and she seated herself on the broad windowseat at the end of the corridor. "Where are you from?"

"San Diego."

"If you went to a big city high school you're going to find it different here. I know. We moved here from New York City three years ago," Cory said.

"I think people are the same everywhere."

"Let me clue you in on something. Don't sound off about California or compare the schools. At first I bragged about New York all the time, and the kids practically ostracized me. It took me a while to catch on. Even if you consider this the remote edge of civilization, don't let on." She pushed a blond lock of hair into place. "I saw you riding to school with Chris Taber. Is he a friend of yours?"

"He's our neighbor."

"Wow, you're lucky. Chris is a great guy. He's co-captain of the hockey team, too." Cory seemed impressed.

"He never told me that," I said.

"You'll find things are pretty slow here in the winter. But when the warm weather comes, the wealthy people open their summer homes and the weekend vacationers start flocking here. It's a whole new scene then—the town is crawling with fantastic guys."

"Well, I'm hoping to keep in touch with my boyfriend in San Diego. I'm planning to spend part of the summer there if I can earn enough money for air fare."

"You'll miss the best time if you go away. The hotels and the top restaurants book big name stars and the town plans all kinds of entertainment for the summer people—art festivals, carnivals, international boat races."

"It must be exciting after being snowed in all winter. But I really want to go visit my friends in California; I'm not sure I'll be here," Robin explained.

"It's easy to find a job in the summer, too. I've worked in a souvenir shop for the past two summers."

"I have a job. I'll be working at Neuman Florist."

"That's great! You lucked out. Have you met Jeffrey Neuman?"

I laughed. "I certainly did."

"What's so funny?" Cory asked.

"I don't think Jeffrey approves of me. He wanted to hire a boy for the job."

"The Neumans are important people in this town. The family goes back for generations and some of their importance has rubbed off on Jeffrey. But you have to admit he's good-looking."

"I'll agree with you on that."

"I think he'd make a great Gothic hero with those dark good looks and those deep brown eyes," Cory said.

"He has all the arrogance of a Gothic hero, too. I think Chris is a lot easier to get along with."

"Chris is the Paddington Bear type. Nothing mysterious about him at all. Now, Jeffrey is another story. He's the assistant director of the junior class production of *Fiddler on the Roof* this spring. I'm in the chorus." Cory shrugged her shoulders. "What I really wanted was a leading part. I would have made a great Tzeitel."

"The chorus is important, too. Every time I see *Fiddler on the Roof* I go around humming the songs for days."

Cory stood up. "There goes the bell. Our next class is world history."

We got up and I followed her to class. The morning went well. Cory seemed to know everybody and most of the kids she introduced me to were friendly. The teachers were helpful and not at all weird like Chris pretended they were. I made a mental note never to take him too seriously.

48

At noon, in the cafeteria, we looked for Rae and Mariann but didn't see them. Chris stopped by our table. "I have hockey practice after school, so I won't be able to take you home. Sorry about that. Take bus Number 34 out by the bus loop—it'll drop you off right in front of your house."

"Thanks, Chris, we'll do okay," I replied.

"Would you like to go skating on the river tonight?" he asked. "A thaw is predicted later in the week and it might end the skating for the season."

"Sure," I answered," but I haven't got any ice skates."

"You can borrow my sister's. I'll pick you up around seven."

"Some girls have all the luck!" Tiffany Lansing exclaimed when Chris left. She was a short, pudgy girl with horn-rimmed glasses. "I wish he'd ask me to go skating. There's a full moon tonight." She threw back her head and howled at the ceiling.

The thought of Tiffany gliding over the ice with Chris, who was easily six feet tall, set us all to laughing.

"New girls are a novelty and all the boys try to date them," Tiffany added. "Do you think if I changed schools I'd be a novelty?"

"Tiffany, you'd be a novelty at any school," Cory replied.

I could tell everyone liked Tiffany. She was good-natured. "Well, we all have our little fantasies," she sighed.

In the afternoon, between classes, I looked for Rae but I didn't see her. I began to worry. I had to tell her about taking the bus home. At the end of sixth period I saw Mariann in the hall. "What happened to Rae?"

"She said she didn't feel well this morning and she went down to the nurse's office. I checked there later to see how she was, and the nurse said she'd driven her home."

I had been afraid something like that would happen. Rae panicked in situations that called attention to her. I remembered the Christmas pageant at church when she was five years old. She ran off the stage in her angel costume when the curtain went up. At the Girl Scout mother-and-daughter banquet one year she was scheduled to deliver the welcoming speech to the mothers, but she turned deathly pale and had to leave the table before the program began. Just last fall she had turned down an invitation to represent our school at a student art show in Washington. I had substituted for Rae on so many occasions I just took it for granted she would never follow through.

When I got home from school, my mother looked up from her desk, gave a shrug of resignation, and pointed to the bedroom. I found Rae lying across her bed reading a magazine. She gave me a look of brooding resentment. "I know what you're thinking but I was really sick. I threw up in the bathroom."

I sat down on the bed. "Rae, you know you have to go to school. Why don't you make up your mind to make the best of it?"

Her voice had a worried sound. "I can't stand everyone looking at me, wondering why I limp. They're thinking: Did I have an accident? Am I getting over a broken ankle? I'm afraid they'll ask and I'll have to tell them I was born this way." She began to cry and I ached for her. We had been through this so many times before.

"Rae, I never told you before, but when I was little I used to wish I had a limp."

She looked astonished. "Why would you want that?"

"I wanted to be like you so I could share everything with you—the painful experiences, the attention you got from Mom and Dad, all the hurt you felt."

"Did it show that much?" Rae asked.

"Sometimes it did," I answered.

"You wouldn't handle it any different than I did, Robin."

"Remember the night Chris told us about his friend in the wheelchair and how popular he is? I hope I'd handled it like he does if I was handicapped."

"He has to be a very special person. I'm not strong like that. I can't reach out to people. They have to come to me."

"We're all afraid of being rejected. But I think we're going to like the new school. The kids are friendly and I feel comfortable with some of them already," I said.

Rae shook her head. "It's different for you. You make friends easily."

"Don't you like Mariann? She seems friendly."

"She's all right. After today she'll probably think I'm a wimp."

"Give the school a chance. It won't seem so strange after a few days," I consoled her.

While we were eating supper the phone rang. It was Mariann asking about Rae. She looked pleased when she came back to the table.

"Mariann asked me to help her paint the scenery tomorrow for *Fiddler on the Roof*. The boy who was helping her is starting wrestling practice."

I breathed a sigh of relief. That took care of getting her to school tomorrow. "See, Mariann doesn't think you're a wimp, after all." I went to the refrigerator and got out the ice cream for the apple pie. "I'm going ice-skating with Chris tonight."

"You've never ice-skated in your life." Rae sounded jealous.

"Yes, but Chris doesn't know that."

"He'll find out soon enough."

"I'm not going to turn down a date with him just because I've never ice-skated."

"What about Kevin? You're getting over him awfully fast," Rae said.

"He hasn't even written to me."

My mother cut the pie. "Honey, some boys don't like to write letters. I don't think I've had a dozen letters from your brother since he went away to school. He'd rather pick up the phone and make a call."

"Reach out and touch someone," Rae sang, and added, "collect."

I finished my pie, thinking of all those extra calories I didn't need. I hoped I'd burn off some of them ice-skating. As Rae and I were finishing the dishes, I heard the high-pitched sound of the snow-mobile coming down the road. I ran to the door and waved to Chris I'd be right out. I wasn't going to expose him to my mother and Rae again.

"You haven't washed the silver yet," Rae called.

"Sorry about that. I'll do the dishes alone tomorrow night."

As I stepped outside, Chris shouted above the roar of the motor, "We're going downriver to Logan's Ferry. They keep about a mile of the river cleared off for skating, and if we get cold we can go into Archie's."

I climbed in back and put my arms tightly around Chris. "Who's Archie?" I shouted back.

"It's a hangout for skaters." We followed a path of moonlit snow as we descended to the river. Tiffany was right. A full moon rode the winter sky, its light so bright I could see a field of pines just ahead under a mantle of snow. I smelled wood smoke in the air, rising in plumes from the chimneys of the houses we passed. Everything seemed silvered and mellowed by the moon's rays.

As we neared Logan's Ferry, blazing wood fires penetrated the darkness, and I could see the skaters gliding and whirling about on the ice. Music piped out from some hidden source spiked the frosty air. We joined a cluster of snowmobiles parked alongside a cement block building that Chris identified as Archie's.

"My sister Beth's skates are a size eight," he said. "If they don't fit, I can rent you a pair inside."

"I wear a size seven but with heavy socks they

should be fine. I have to level with you, Chris," I admitted. "I've never ice-skated."

"That's no problem. I'll teach you."

"You never told me you were co-captain of the hockey team."

"I'm giving autographs later," Chris joked.

"Everyone roller-skates in California and I'm almost a pro on a skateboard, but I've never been near an ice rink."

"This is no rink, Robin. The St. Lawrence River is frozen all the way to the Atlantic Ocean. Come on, we'll change into our skates inside where it's warm," Chris said as he led the way toward Archie's.

When we stepped inside, the warm air enveloped us, smelling of wet mittens, grilled onions, and sheepskin boots. The place was jammed with kids stomping about on the wooden floor or crowded into the booths drinking Cokes and eating Archieburgers, which Chris explained were a specialty of the house. A beat-up jukebox in the corner pulsed with rock music, and a few couples were dancing in their heavy socks.

Low wooden benches flanked the wall, and I sat down while Chris helped me with my skates, his big hands pulling the laces firmly and tying them. He was making me feel special again. I felt such a rush of tenderness toward him, I wanted to reach out and touch him. He pulled me to my feet. I wobbled trying to get my balance, and I leaned against him as we clumped through the snow to the river.

As I went slipping and sliding over the ice I felt

the strength of his arms holding me upright. My ankles kept turning over, but Chris was reassuring. "Just glide forward, one foot at a time. I won't let you fall." Skaters sped by us as I teetered awkwardly, clinging to Chris like a drowning person.

"It's not at all like roller skating," I complained. "I can't keep my balance."

"You're catching on," Chris said after we had circled the skating area several times. I abandoned myself to his rhythm—a little shakily, I'll admit—but we moved together as one. The only sound was the *click, swish* of our skates. Jeffrey skated by with a girl in a red skating outfit. If he recognized me he didn't let on.

"Do you want to rest?" Chris asked. There were no skaters at the far end of the ice, where the plows had pushed the snow into huge piles that reminded me of pictures of the moon's craggy surface. It seemed as desolate as the moon, too, so far away from the skaters and the music.

"Did you ever see the moon so close?" Chris asked softly. His face was shadowed in the moonlight and he smelled of wood smoke and the cold. Suddenly he kissed me, his lips soft and smooth on mine. I drew my breath in sharply in surprise. I don't know why. I had been waiting for him to kiss me ever since that afternoon we tumbled in the snow under the bridge.

"I happen to be Aquarius"—he smiled—"and you know how impulsive we are."

"I'm Scorpio and you know how conservative we are," I replied. I lost my cool for a moment. I felt shaken and a little breathless.

It was snowing lightly and he brushed some snow-flakes from my cheek. "Scorpios are also romantic and fiercely possessive." Then he kissed me again. I wanted him to go on holding me close. It seemed such a natural thing to do, out under the shimmering stars with only the moon watching us.

I clung to him, and not just to keep from falling on my skates. I knew I was beginning to care for him and there might not be any future in it. Maybe Tiffany was right and the boys gave new girls a rush —testing them out, bragging about it the next day.

Later we went back to Archie's, found an empty booth, and ordered bowls of chili. We held hands across the table as we waited. "I didn't tell you I'm starting a job at Neuman Florist on Saturday. I don't know if I'll have a lot of spare time," I said.

"Then we'll have to make the most of this week. I'm playing my last hockey game of the season tomorrow night. I hope you can come and watch us play."

"I'll be there." I could have told him raging pneumonia wouldn't keep me away.

"There's a party tomorrow night after the game at Monty Andrews's. Would you like to come? We hope it will be a victory party."

"Sure, I'm the original party girl," I said happily.

"Spoken like a true Scorpio," Chris smiled. "If the cold weather holds, I'd like to take you cross-country skiing this weekend."

"I skied at Aspen last winter with my parents. We went there for my birthday." I felt good that at least I knew how to do one winter sport.

"Are you trying to tell me you're pretty good?

That's fine. I won't have to hold you up." Chris smiled at me warmly and then he asked, "How is your sister adjusting to school?"

Rae again. Chris was interested in her. Maybe I was just a fill-in.

The waitress brought steaming bowls of chili and little packages of crackers. I broke the cellophane off the crackers before I answered, "She was sick and the nurse had to bring her home second period."

"With her disposition, no wonder she got sick."

"She wasn't always like this. Lately she's more conscious of her handicap. Moving here hasn't helped, and my parents' divorce . . ." I hadn't wanted to mention that. My face felt stiff and I stirred my chili, hoping Chris wouldn't pursue the subject.

He must have understood. He said quietly, "We'll have to try to get her involved. It's a small school but there are plenty of activities."

"Mariann talked her into painting the scenery for the musical," I said.

"That's a start. She'll feel better about school in a few days."

The moon rode higher in the sky and the wind blew colder as we rode home. I hoped my face wouldn't chap. I was worried my skin wouldn't adapt to the cold. I had the kind of skin that always had problems—sunburn, windburn, everything.

When we said good night he didn't kiss me again. He left the snowmobile running until I was in the door. I wasn't quite sure about Chris. I always knew where I stood with Kevin, but then I had known him longer. Chris seemed to like me, but he could be dating a dozen other girls for all I knew. He might be the Warren Beatty of the junior class.

My mother and Rae were still up when I came in. "It's nearly eleven o'clock," my mother said. "I think you had better confine your dates to weekends, Robin."

"There's a party tomorrow night at Monty Andrews's to celebrate the end of the hockey season. I already told Chris I'd go with him," I said.

"Kevin called tonight—if you had been home you could have talked to him," my mother told me.

"Kevin! Did he say he would call back?" I asked excitedly.

"No. He wanted to tell you he has a job this summer as a surveyor's apprentice—he's going to Alaska."

"Alaska! Then I won't see him at all this summer! That's just great!"

"It's a wonderful opportunity for him," my mother said gently.

"How did he get a job like that?"

"His uncle's construction firm has contracts in Alaska. He talked with Rae for a while."

"What did he say to you, Rae?" I asked.

"He wanted to know where you were. I told him you were snowmobiling with a boy you met at school."

"Thanks a lot!"

"Kevin said he would be balancing tripods on the top of hundred-foot water towers and hacking his way through virgin forests. He really seemed excited about the job. He said he was going to visit here this summer during the international boat races but he wouldn't be able to now," Rae said.

"Sure," I answered. "Hurrah for Kevin!"

In my bedroom I took Kevin's class ring off my chain and put it in my jewelry box. I might as well send it back to him. Maybe Kevin could give it to a girl in Alaska.

CHAPTER FIVE

Cory asked me to go to the night hockey game with her. Her boyfriend, Dave, was a senior and would be playing his last game. She was being sentimental about it.

My mother reluctantly drove me over to Cory's house. "This is your last date on a school night this week, Robin. I'm glad you're making friends, but your schoolwork is important, too. It's so easy for you to get involved in too many activities."

"That's me," I replied. "Always in the fast track."

"I just wish your sister was as outgoing."

"She could have come to the game with us. I asked her," I said.

"Was she invited to the party, too?"

"No, but I could have arranged it."

My mother fell silent. She was shoveling guilt on me again. Sometimes a maverick thought pushed at me. Did she love Rae more because my sister had a stronger need of her? Some of the excitement of looking forward to the game and the party was dulled as I thought of Rae staying home while I was having a good time.

I met Cory's parents, and Cory and I walked over to the rink. She lived right around the corner from the school. The players were warming up under the lights and I picked Chris out right away. He was Number 14. He looked so big in his padded orange-and-black uniform.

Cory had brought along a woolen blanket because the temperature was in the twenties. We wrapped ourselves up in it to keep warm while we sat in the stands. I didn't know much about hockey, but I screamed and clapped when Cory did and kept my eyes on Number 14 all the time.

"Chris plays defense," Cory explained. "I think he's spectacular. We're lucky he has another year to play for the school. I wouldn't be surprised if he makes the All-County team."

The team won 4–3, and we joined the crowd of kids running out on the ice to congratulate the players. We couldn't get near Chris and Dave. Then Chris saw me, and he broke away and skated toward me. I suddenly felt shy having him seek me out in front of everyone.

"Thanks for coming, Robin."

"Congratulations. This is a super way to end the season."

"I'm glad for Dave's sake. It's a good feeling when your last game for the school ends in a victory." He looked around. "Didn't Rae come, or isn't she a hockey fan?"

I felt a little stab of jealousy again. "No, she didn't make it."

61

"You're still coming to the party tonight?"

"Over my mother's protests. She doesn't like me out on school nights. I'm going over to Cory's house now."

"I'll pick you up there."

Chris and Dave came along in the jeep about nine o'clock, and we drove through the village streets to Monty's. A small sign by the sidewalk in front of his house announced, FRANK ANDREWS, M.D.

The party was in the paneled family room, complete with a pool table, stereo, and TV. Mrs. Andrews had arranged the food buffet-style in the kitchen—pizza, cold cuts, salads, and a large cake decorated with a hockey player wearing orange and black, the school colors. It looked as if it was going to be a good party.

Chris and Dave said they were starving after the game and joined the other kids filling up their plates at the table. I thought the paper plates would collapse under all the food Chris and Dave piled on. "This is just our first helping," Chris explained.

Ahead of me I saw Jeffrey with a girl I recognized as one of the cheerleaders at the game. She was still wearing her heavy orange sweater and black skirt. Her dark hair fell to her waist. She and Jeff looked as if they belonged together. Even as a new student I could pick out the winners, the kids who had everything—brains, poise, and personality.

Later Chris and I danced. During the slow dances I found a comfortable spot on his shoulder, and it seemed so natural for him to be holding me close.

Then someone put on a tape of the latest disco hit. Without a thought I moved away from Chris and started dancing. Chris just stood and looked at me. Laughing and clapping, some of the boys formed a circle around me and I really revved it up, dancing with all the abandon of Clara Bow in a late-night movie. I didn't need any encouragement when it came to dancing.

Tom Smith, one of the hockey players, stepped forward and started dancing opposite me. He was really good, and I was enjoying myself.

"Quite an exhibition," Chris remarked, his face serious, when the music ended and I turned back to him. I was out of breath and my face was flushed. I couldn't tell if he was criticizing me or not. Maybe I shouldn't have grabbed the limelight at my first party; I should have laid back and observed the tribal customs of the natives.

Someone called from the doorway, "Phil's car is stuck in the snow. How about you guys giving us a hand?" The room nearly emptied as all of the boys and some of the girls went outside.

I studied some photographs on the wall. One was a college graduation picture from the fifties, and I assumed it was Dr. Andrews's class. I had met him when we arrived at the party, but I couldn't pick him out in the photograph.

"Hi, I'm Stephanie Ryan." I turned to see the girl who'd been talking to Jeffrey. "I'm in your world history class but I'm afraid you don't remember me. It's hard to sort people out when you're new in school."

"I'm working on it. I can barely keep the teachers straight."

"Jeffrey says you're going to be working with him," Stephanie said.

"Then Jeffrey does know I'm here. I was beginning to think he didn't recognize me."

"Oh, he knows you're here, all right. He told me all about you and how you moved here from San Diego. In fact, I'm a little jealous."

"You don't have to be jealous, believe me. I'm not his type."

"I hear there's someone back in San Diego."

"Did Cory announce it over the public address system at school? She was the only one I told," I said.

She laughed. "It's a small school, Robin. News gets around fast. We're all curious about new students. We don't get too many of them. Besides, you were wearing a class ring on your necklace the first day of school."

The conversation was getting personal. I looked around. "I wonder what's keeping the fellows?"

"They're probably standing around outside discussing girls. Phil's Pinto can't be stuck that badly in the snow. Those hulks could pick it up and carry it."

The boys came in finally and I saw Jeffrey walking toward us. "Hello, Robin." He looked me over as carefully as a weight-guesser at a carnival.

"Hello, Jeffrey." Why did anyone so miserable have to be so good-looking?

"Quite the life of the party, aren't you?" He was making fun of me. "I've never seen a more exuberant performance."

"Just trying to liven up the party," I quipped,

and quickly realized it was the wrong thing to say. I was on probation, and I was making the party sound dull. To make matters worse, Chris had come up behind me and probably heard me say it.

Jeffrey raised an eyebrow. "You think the party's boring?"

I felt my color mount. "Of course not. It's a good party." But the harm had been done. Chris handed me a Coke he brought over from the refreshment table. "I'm going to play a game of pool with Dave."

Someone called to Stephanie and Jeffrey and they moved away, leaving me alone. I couldn't stand alone in the middle of the room. There was nothing to do but go over and watch Chris play pool. He acted as if I wasn't there.

When the game was over, Chris walked over to the wall and hung up his cue stick. I followed him. "Look, did I do something wrong?"

"That crack about livening up the party won't win you any popularity contests. Monty's parents went all out to put on a good party for the team."

"I know they did and I'm sorry I made that remark. I didn't mean it that way. Jeffrey was needling me."

"Maybe you think we're a bunch of squares up here in the north country," Chris said angrily.

"I didn't mean to show off. It's just the way I am. You're blowing it all out of proportion."

"I told you I always say what I think."

"Even if you sound stupid?" I was making him angry but I didn't care.

He looked at his watch. "It's a quarter to eleven.

I'd better get you home before your mother throws a fit."

We drove through the village without talking, dropped Cory off, then Dave, and headed along the river road for my house. I sat close to the car door, as far away from Chris as possible. He turned into our driveway and parked. Then he turned off the car lights and the radio. The silence seemed dark and heavy.

He turned to me. "Robin, I'm sorry. Let's not quarrel. I guess I wanted you all to myself tonight. I was jealous when I saw that you were the center of attention and dancing with Tom."

I wanted to hold him and tell him I understood but I knew I had to settle something with him tonight. "No one owns me, Chris. When I'm out with people, I'm right in the center of things. That's the way I am. If you can't accept that, maybe we shouldn't see each other anymore."

"I don't want to change you. I've never felt this way about a girl before."

"I care for you, too, Chris but I have to be free to be myself."

"Then you'll have to accept some things about me, too. I have a quick temper and you already know I have a big mouth."

"It doesn't sound too promising for a relationship," I said.

"Let's give it a chance. I take it as a good sign that you've stopped wearing the class ring around your neck."

"Maybe it was tarnishing my neck."

"I don't think so." In the moonlight I could see

66

Chris grin. "I have my faults but I'm also lovable, affectionate, and good to my mother."

"A regular Paddington Bear," I murmured.

"What was that?"

"Just a little joke between Cory and me." It was impossible to stay angry with Chris. I leaned toward him, and just as he kissed me my mother turned on the porch light, her signal that it was time for me to come into the house.

CHAPTER
SIX

I drove to the airport Friday night to pick up my brother. Mac came striding off the ramp in a heavy sheepskin coat and a dark cap on his curly hair. His face was strongly handsome. He gave me a bear hug. "Hi, Rob. Have you reorganized the School Board and taken over the Chamber of Commerce?"

"I'm working on it." I touched his coat. "Where did you get the winter threads?"

"I borrowed them from my roommate who's from Vermont. I also borrowed his boots, gloves, and long johns. I knew it was going to be really cold here."

"How was your flight?"

"When the elderly woman sitting next to me found out I was studying to be a doctor, I had to listen to her sinus problems all the way from Atlanta." He collected his baggage and we walked out to the parking lot. I handed him the car keys.

"How's Mom?" Mac asked.

"She amazes me. Remember how Dad wouldn't let her do anything around the house? Now she's painting and hammering and sawing."

68

"How is she really? Emotionally?"

"She's hurting but she keeps it all inside. I wish she'd talk about it sometimes. I hear her up at night when she can't sleep," I told him.

"She will when she's ready. Maybe it's too painful for her to talk about it now. And Rae?"

"Rae is having a few problems."

"Are you still running interference for her?"

"I'm used to doing it," I admitted.

"Rob, it's an admirable trait to be sensitive and caring, but sometimes you have to be a tough cookie. It's best for your sake as well as hers."

I studied my hands. "I'm making friends, I'm starting a job, I like the new school—but when I see Rae so unhappy . . ." My voice trailed off.

"You'll be in college next year and you won't be around to throw a lifeline to her when she thinks she can't cope."

"I know. I wish you weren't so far away. You help keep things in perspective," I said.

"I wish I could help more."

We drove for a while in silence. When our house came in sight Mac said, "Grandfather's house was one of the first built around here. According to the the local historian that was around 1800."

"I can believe that," I admitted gloomily.

"The Onondaga and Iroquois Indians used this area as a hunting ground and later the War of 1812 caused a lot of destruction along the river."

"Some of the shots they fired must have gone right through my bedroom walls. It's certainly drafty in there."

Mac laughed. "Maybe I can do something about it this winter."

"The house is a real clunker. You should have seen it when we moved in," I said drearily.

"I remember it from my vacations when I was a kid. I thought it was Shangri-la. Nothing to do but swim, fish, and ride the tour boat with Grandpa."

"Well, Shangri-la has fallen on hard times."

Mom was waiting with a roast beef dinner for us, and later Mac made plans for the work he would do around the house over the weekend. It was good to have him around. I was almost sorry I had to start my new job the next day.

I set my alarm for seven o'clock the next morning. That would give me time to dress, have breakfast, and walk to work. When I awoke the sun was coming up and the icicles were dripping outside my bedroom window. This could be the thaw Chris said was expected this week. As I walked to work I was thinking how I was enjoying the snow. It was a new experience, but it was exciting, too, to think of the river coming to life and to be able to explore the islands.

The warm, moist, earthy smell met me again when I stepped inside the greenhouse. No one was in sight so I headed for the office. Since last week, the buds of the Easter lilies had swelled and they looked like green exclamation points jutting out from the stem. The tulips and the daffodils were still tightly budded and gave no hint of the colors within.

"Good morning," someone said behind me, and I

jumped. It was Jeffrey carrying a bag of peat moss on his shoulder. Even in patched jeans and a faded sweatshirt he had class. He set the bag down on a bench. "Would you like a quick tour of the place before you start work?"

"That sounds like a good idea." I was wary, although I saw no hint of the arrogance he had shown the first day.

He indicated the rows of potted plants. "We have nearly ten thousand plants we're growing for the Easter trade. Easter is one of the busiest days in our business, followed by Mother's Day and Memorial Day." He led the way into another greenhouse. I stood in awe at the profusion of lush tropical plants, some of them ten to twelve feet tall. It was like walking into a jungle world where tropical vegetation threatened to shut out the sun.

"We have varieties of orchids here from Brazil, Burma, and the Philippines," he explained.

We walked through a narrow corridor to still another greenhouse, where six women were working. "Our transplanting is done here." The women's hands flew as they took tiny seedlings, made holes in containers of soil, and deftly positioned the little plants.

"They're planting petunias and marigolds that will be ready for the market in May. Your job will be to keep these women supplied with flats filled with a mixture of soil, peat moss, and vermiculite. The mixture is in a pile at the far end of the greenhouse."

The wooden flats were about three inches high.

71

Jeffrey showed me how to use a trowel to fill them with soil, then smooth the surface evenly. "You'll have to work fast. Do you think you can handle it?"

"Of course I can handle it. Will the women come and pick up their flats?"

"Oh, no. You have to take the flats to them." Did I get a glint of a smirk on his face? He was just waiting for me to complain. I'd show him!

He left and I started working. It took about five big scoops of soil to fill each flat. As I piled the flats on top of each other, I figured six would be all I could carry at one time. They were heavy as I carried them, trying to hurry over the slippery floor.

"Thanks, honey," called a big blond woman working at the transplanting table. "Keep those flats coming!"

I hurried back and began filling more flats. Would I be able to keep up? I worked as fast as I could, but the women used the flats up as fast as I filled them. The hardest part was carrying them the full length of the greenhouse. The warm, moist air that seemed so pleasant when I arrived this morning now seemed humid. My sweater itched and I felt sweaty. I was sure my face was smudged but I couldn't take time to go to the restroom.

I glanced at my watch; it was only ten-fifteen. I should have applied for a job at a fast food restaurant or as a checkout girl at a supermarket. Better yet, I should be home curled up in a chair reading a book. My mother said I didn't *have* to work. It all started with the wild idea to fly to California to see Kevin this summer. Now Kevin was dreaming of Alaska while I was slaving in here. I knew Jeff was lurking around watching me and waiting for me to give up.

Mr. Neuman came by. "How are you doing, Robin?"

I straightened my aching back. "I'm keeping up. Just barely."

He frowned. "Don't tell me you're carrying those flats by hand! Didn't Jeff tell you to use the high-rise cart?"

I gave him a blank look. "What high-rise cart?"

He disappeared and came back pushing a narrow cart with three tiers of shelves. "No wonder you have trouble keeping up with the women. I can't understand why Jeff didn't tell you."

I can, I thought wearily. He wants me to quit.

Mr. Neuman helped me fill the flats until the cart was full, and I rolled it easily down the aisle to the transplanting tables.

At noon I saw the women sitting down with their bagged lunches and thermos bottles. I had planned on going home for lunch, but now I learned from Mr. Neuman we only had a half-hour for lunch, I could never make it home and back in time. I realized how hungry I was. I put a quarter in the soft drink machine near the office and sat down to sip a root beer. It would have to last me until the four-thirty closing time. My mother, Rae, and Mac were probably having hot roast beef sandwiches this noon from last night's roast. My stomach growled just because I was thinking about it.

The blond woman came down the aisle. "Honey, why don't you join us? You don't have to sit here alone."

I was embarrassed. "I didn't bring lunch."

"You poor child! Now don't you worry. I always pack extra sandwiches for our coffee break."

"I'm really not hungry," I lied.

She took my arm and propelled me down the aisle in front of her. "What's your name, honey? I'm Grace."

"Robin."

"Robin came without her lunch this morning," Grace explained to her co-workers. As a result, I ended up with four half-sandwiches, an apple, a brownie, and a chocolate chip cookie. Mrs. Hessler and Mrs. Ruffle were two grandmotherly types. The younger women introduced themselves as Stella, Doris, and Irene. When I satisfied their curiosity as to the size of my family and where I was from, they settled back to discussing their families, their favorite soap operas, and the high cost of living.

When I finished eating, I leaned back against a pile of burlap bags and closed my eyes. The sun was warm and the womens' voices droned on. The next thing I knew, Grace was leaning over, gently shaking me. "Robin, it's time to go back to work."

I sat up, horrified. "I didn't mean to fall asleep. Did anyone see me? I mean, Mr. Neuman or his son?"

"Just Jeffrey." She smiled. "He was passing through. He said you looked as if you were all worn out."

Without a word I got up and hurried back to the high-rise cart and the pile of soil. I had probably fallen asleep with my mouth wide open, even snoring

74

a little. Worn out! That's just what Jeffrey was hoping for. Then he could tell me it was a boy's job and too hard for a girl. I attacked the pile of soil with a vengeance.

I could see the other employees watering the plants and spraying for insect control, but Jeffrey kept out of sight. Maybe his father had reprimanded him.

An elderly workman stopped by and introduced himself as Pop Wegman. He said he had worked for the Neumans for forty-two years. "I knew your grandfather. He was a real river man. He knew the river like the palm of his hand—every shoal, every rock. As a fishing guide he was one of the best in the north country."

"I hope we can talk about my grandfather some time," I said.

"I have some photographs of the old tour boats with your grandfather as skipper. I'll bring them in and give them to you. I'm happy your family has come back here to live."

"Thank you, Mr. Wegman—for the pictures and the welcome."

As he walked away I thought, *Did I belong here? Had fate manipulated our lives so we would return to the old family home?*

I was relieved that Grace offered me a ride home from work. We talked on the way. "You put in a hard day's work, honey," she said. "Some people think greenhouse work is easy, that all you have to do is watch the flowers grow, but it's hard, back-breaking work. Why don't you ask for a job in the retail store?"

"I didn't know there was one," I answered.

"It's at the far side of the greenhouses. They make and sell flower arrangements and corsages and handle special orders for holidays, banquets, weddings, and funerals."

"That sounds interesting. I was hired for the greenhouse work, but maybe when I'm here longer I can switch."

"You'll earn your money," Grace reassured me.

"I'm sure I will," I said.

When I walked in the door, Mac was busy laying brown-and-rust tweed carpeting in the kitchen. My mother had noticed a carpet sale in the paper and they had gone into town to purchase it. "Not bad," I said. "It improves the kitchen, makes it seem warmer.

"How did your new job go, Robin?" my mother asked.

"I made it through the day." I could have wallowed in their sympathy and told them about the dirty trick Jeffrey had played on me, but it wouldn't have helped my problem. That was between Jeffrey and me.

"The first day is always the hardest," Mac commented. "Do you think you'll like the work?"

"Let's say it's challenging."

"Mac's driving us over to Uncle Bob's this evening. Do you want to come, too?" my mother asked.

"I'm going to take a hot bath and watch TV, if I can stay awake. I've got dozens of muscles I never knew I had and they're all aching," I said. Besides, I wanted to be home if Chris called.

My mother took some salad greens out of the refrigerator. "This glass-topped table looked great in California but it looks ridiculous in a country kitchen. Besides, I'm sick of looking at people's legs when I eat. Mac went out in the barn yesterday and he said there's an oak trestle table there. I'm thinking of bringing it in here and selling this one if I can find anyone to buy it."

After my bath I fell asleep on the top of my bed and didn't get up until the next morning. My mother had thrown a comforter over me before she went to bed. Even if Chris had called, I wouldn't have heard the phone. My muscles were still sore Sunday morning. I moaned and groaned as I sat around in my robe eating a leisurely breakfast and reading the paper.

Chris phoned before dinner. "The snow is going fast and this might be our last chance to do some cross-country skiing. Should I bring along my sister's skis for you, or do you own a pair?"

"No, I don't own any. We always rented them. I hope I can meet your sister sometime and thank her," I said.

"She's away at college but she'll be home over Easter."

"I'll bring my camera along. I'd like to take some pictures of the islands." I really wanted to take some pictures of Chris for myself and also to send to Sue and Penny. They could eat their hearts out instead of feeling sorry for me because Kevin was going to Alaska and would probably forget all about me.

"What time are you having dinner?"

"One o'clock," I said.

"I'll pick you up around two. We can get a few hours of skiing in before dark."

"Who was that?" my mother asked when I hung up.

"I'm going skiing with Chris after dinner."

"I thought you were tired," Mother said.

"She decided she's not that tired," Mac said. "Come on, Robin, get dressed and give me a hand with the trestle table."

The barn was dim and shadowy and cold. Piles of furniture—beds, dressers, desks, lamps, and chairs—filled one side of the barn. Farm tools hung from the walls and bushel baskets of dishes, books, pots, and pans stood on the floor.

"Where did Grandma put all this furniture?" I asked. "It never would have fit in that little house."

"Some of it was probably handed down to her by her parents or relatives who passed away, and she just stored it out here."

I had a strange feeling as I stood there, as if the ghosts of those who had treasured these possessions were silently watching us. A chill ran through me. Were we intruders or were we caretakers who would cherish these possessions? That old-fashioned desk. How many times had my grandmother sat there writing letters to her loved ones? I could picture my grandfather resting in the golden oak chair with the scrolled back and looking out over the river he loved.

Mac pointed to a long table. Thick polished boards formed the top. "Here's the trestle table. Want to give me a hand with it?" I helped him pull it out into a clear space on the barn floor. It was unbelievably heavy. "I'm going to need some help carrying it through the snow to the house. I'd better wait until that boyfriend of yours comes by."

"He'll be glad to help."

Mac lifted one side of the table. "I hope he's strong."

"Wait until you see him. He's bigger than you," I said.

While Mac searched for chairs, I prowled among the pieces of dusty furniture, opening dresser drawers filled with clothing, towels, and tablecloths. I opened the lid of an old wooden blanket chest and under several flannel sheet blankets, I found another wedding ring quilt carefully wrapped in plastic.

"Mom was right!" I exclaimed. "She said Grandma probably planned on sewing quilts for both of us girls." The other quilt we had found wasn't finished yet but this one was, in a design formed by tiny blocks of blue on a white background. "This must be my quilt. Grandma knew blue was my favorite color," I said excitedly.

"Bring it in the house. It's too damp to leave it out here," Mac said.

I was so pleased to have found the quilt. It was almost as if Grandma had wanted me to find it. I hugged it to me, smelling the faint scent of cedar.

I found some other things to bring back to the house, a porcelain clock with hand-painted sprays of flowers and a Victorian-style mirror I wanted for my bedroom. Mac found a schoolroom wall clock. "I'd like this for the office I hope to have someday. It will give it a touch of class."

"Take it with you, Dr. Thomas."

"I'll carry it back with me on the plane. I remember it hanging in the kitchen."

When we came back to the house, Rae pounced on the quilt. She tore off the plastic. "The wedding ring quilt! It's beautiful! It will look great with my white furniture."

"Wait a minute," I said. "What makes you think it's yours?"

She seemed surprised I even asked. "The colors will go with my room—I can use it as a bedspread. The other quilt isn't finished yet."

"I'm the oldest and I'm sure Grandma made the first quilt for me. She knew blue was my favorite color."

"I think Robin is right," my mother said quietly. "We'll all help finish the other quilt—it will be fun working on it together. It won't take long. The pieces are all cut out."

"That's not fair, Robin," Rae insisted. "You have the biggest bedroom and the view of the river."

"You chose your bedroom yourself."

Mac caught my eye, and he was shaking his head as if signaling me not to give in.

Rae scowled. "You just wanted to get in the barn and get first choice of everything. You'll probably want to keep the porcelain clock, too."

"No, you can have it. The mirror, too."

Mac spoke up. "Nothing stopped you from joining us, Rae. The barn is full of interesting antiques if you want to go out and look around."

"Sure, Mac. You're always on Robin's side."

"Stop acting like a brat, Rae," Mac said. "What's gotten into you lately?"

"You want the quilt for your hope chest, Robin! Well, hope chests are old-fashioned, in case you don't know it!"

"I wasn't thinking of a hope chest, but maybe Grandma planned the quilts as wedding gifts."

Tears welled up in Rae's eyes. "You're all so sure I won't get married. Maybe I won't but I don't care!"

My mother looked pained. I had seen that expression before, when she had to explain to Rae she couldn't take ballet lessons when she was six years old.

I felt uncomfortable. I had a great afternoon ahead of me skiing with Chris. I liked my new school and the future looked good to me. If Rae wasn't able to cope, it wasn't her fault. I sighed. "All right, if it means so much to you, take the quilt."

"Robin!" Mac's voice was sharp.

"It's only a quilt."

"It's the principle of the thing. That quilt was meant for you!" Mac was disgusted with me.

I tried to sound casual. "I'll finish the other one. What's the difference?"

Rae came over and kissed me. "Thanks, Robin. I'll help you with the other quilt. I really do like this one." She paused. "You're not mad at me, are you?"

"Like I said, it's only a quilt."

Mac followed me out into the kitchen and closed the door behind him. "Listen, Robin, you're going to keep running backward to soothe your conscience about Rae, and one of these days she's going to take off and sprint right by you."

I felt miserable having Mac mad at me. "I don't want to talk about it."

"I give up! It's your hang-up, not mine. Just don't let it mess up your life."

CHAPTER
SEVEN

Chris arrived after dinner and helped Mac carry the trestle table in from the barn. They also brought in some pine chairs and a wooden butter churn. My mother went bananas over the churn. "It's a real treasure," she explained. "It was in the woodshed when I lived here as a child. I'm going to put it right here in the corner."

"Rustic chic," Rae commented. "All we need is a cowbell and the Farmers' Almanac hanging on the wall."

"Don't knock it, Rae," Mac replied. "Some of these antiques are valuable. How do you like the table, Robin?"

"I'm undergoing culture shock but I think I'll adjust." I trailed my hand over the wood, mellowed with age. How many years of use and how many polishings had given it the soft patina? I had that strange feeling again as if I had come in contact with the past.

"What are we going to do with this glass-topped

table? It looks so silly in the house now," Mother said.

"Put it in the woodshed for now," Mac said. "Maybe you can have a yard sale later in the year. I have a hunch you're going to bring in more things from the barn."

Chris glanced at his watch. "We'd better get going, Robin, if we want to get in a few hours of skiing before dark. Be sure and dress warmly."

My mother reminded me. "Mac's flight is scheduled for six-thirty—we should leave for the airport by five o'clock. Be sure to be home by then."

"Sure thing. I wouldn't miss seeing the doctor off."

We went outside and Chris helped me on with my skis. We moved out over the snow. Our skis carried us over drifts, along stone fences almost hidden by snow. I was beginning to enjoy the silence of winter, the snow sparkling in the afternoon sun, the air fresh and clear. We discovered round hollows in the snow, and Chris explained that animals had rested there— deer perhaps. The heat of their bodies had melted the snow and left a bowllike depression, lined with ice. Farther on he pointed out the wandering footprints of a hunting fox.

I took several pictures of Chris goofing off on his skis and a serious one with a field of pines in the background. I was sure it would turn out to look like an advertisement for a high-class ski resort. That's the one I would send to Sue and Penny. He took some of me squinting in the sun; I knew they'd turn out terrible.

As we moved silently over the snow, we saw a doe and a buck deer sunning themselves at the edge of the woods. They stood side by side, their heads held high, their coats shining in the sun. They hadn't seen us yet and we stopped. It was a beautiful sight; I was glad to be sharing it with Chris. I reached over and took his hand. For several moments they stood motionless, then the buck swung his head in our direction. Some sound, some movement, must have caught his eye, for with a great bound he whirled toward the trees. The doe followed. In three or four graceful leaps they disappeared into the woods.

"How beautiful," I said softly to Chris. Our eyes met and we smiled in understanding.

After we had been out about an hour, the breeze freshened and it became a wind. The cold was beginning to seep through my clothing, but I didn't want to complain. Then my shivering gave me away. "Are you cold, Robin? I forgot you're not used to our weather yet."

"Maybe we'd better turn back." My knees were stiff from the cold, and I was leaning heavily on the poles to help me along.

"My uncle has a fishing camp not far from here. We can go in and start a fire and get warm before we start back," Chris suggested.

"How will we get in?"

"I know where he keeps the key."

"Will he mind?" I asked.

"He lets my family use it all year round. Some of the best bass fishing in the islands is right offshore.

The camp was really a small rustic cabin made of

logs with a wide, gray stone chimney. Chris took the key out from between the logs and we let ourselves in. It seemed even colder inside, and Chris quickly found some newspapers and kindling to start a blaze in the fireplace. As it caught fire and flared up, he added some white birch logs from a neat pile beside the fireplace.

The furnishings were sparse—a few cupboards, a table and chairs, bunk beds, and an Indian rug before the fireplace. I sat close to the fire warming myself. When Chris was sure the fire had taken hold, he stretched out on the floor beside me with his head in my lap. With my fingertips I traced his eyebrows, his nose, the curve of his lips. He caught my hand and held it against his cheek, still cold from outside.

"How did your job go yesterday?"

"O.K." I'd keep quiet about Jeffrey pulling a fast one on me at the greenhouse. I didn't want Chris mentioning it to him. I asked, "Tell me about Jeffrey. Are you two good friends?"

"Jeff's all right. He's a little conceited but he's not a bad guy. We were close through grade school —same Scout troup, same Little League, and all that stuff. When we got into high school, our interests and our friends changed. I went in heavy for sports and Jeff leaned toward the school paper and the drama club. My friends are the jocks and Jeff hangs out with the VIPs, the kids who get elected to class offices and make the Honor Society."

"Cory told me he's assistant director of the school musical this spring."

"That's the sort of thing he goes in for. Come to think of it, I could be jealous of you working for him. I don't need that kind of competition," Chris said.

"For Pete's sake! That's all I hear from everyone! I'd just as soon date Bigfoot!"

"Ah ha! Yesterday at the greenhouse didn't go too well, did it? We can always give you a job at the marina selling gasoline and bait."

"I don't want to talk about it," I said.

"All right. Be silent, secretive. I don't want to know, anyway." He closed his eyes.

I liked being alone with Chris; I felt relaxed and at peace with the world. I hadn't felt contented in a long time. I smoothed back his hair and wished mine was as curly.

"That feels good," he murmured. "Don't stop."

I wound his hair around my fingers and made little curls. I could imagine his mother making blond ringlets when he was a baby. The room grew warmer and I could feel the chill going out of my body. I thought of the long cold trip back home and wished we could just stay here where it was warm and quiet, with no one to bother us.

I wondered if Chris was asleep, or was he just pretending? As I stared into the fire I found myself becoming drowsy. I fought to stay awake but I dozed off. When I woke up, the flames were making shadows on the wall and the light was darkening outside the window.

"Chris!" I shook him. "We've got to leave! It's getting dark!"

He opened his eyes. "Why did you let me sleep so long?" He looked at his watch. "It's nearly five o'clock."

"I'm in trouble. I promised to get back in time to go to the airport," I said.

"I meant to get you back in time. Your mother will blacklist me now." Chris looked concerned.

"I wanted to say good-bye to Mac. I don't know when I'll see him again."

"I'm sorry. I shouldn't have brought you so far."

"I've never skied in the dark. We might get lost."

"I could find my way back blindfolded. We're late now, so there's no use hurrying."

"Chris, did you plan to bring me here?"

He smiled. "It might have been in the back of my mind. Is there anything wrong with two people who like each other wanting to be alone?" He pulled me down on the rug beside him. I knew I should push him away but being held so closely, so warmly, made me feel that Chris really loved me.

"It's warm in here," he said softly. "Why don't you take off your jacket?"

I was wary. "It's not that warm."

"I've got to take mine off. It must be eighty degrees in here." He took off his jacket, then he reached down and unzipped my parka.

"We've got to get back," I protested, but he slipped my parka off my shoulders.

"I thought you liked me, Robin."

"I do like you, Chris." He drew me to him again and his kiss was lingering. I was alarmed at my feelings, even though a part of me resisted. Maybe Chris was just testing the new girl at school so he could brag about it tomorrow. But I didn't want to believe that. Sealed off from the world in this little cabin, I just wanted Chris to go on kissing me. The shadows on the wall deepened as it grew darker outside.

"I love you," he whispered. I felt such a rush of tenderness.

"We have to start back, Chris," I insisted.

He wouldn't let me go. I felt alarmed, trapped. I pushed at him hard. He looked hurt but he let me go. Without speaking he got up, put on his coat, and went outside. He brought back some snow and threw it on the fire. Steam and smoke rose from the logs. "Let's hit the trail," he said.

I hoped he wasn't angry. "Are you sure the fire is out?"

"Yes, both of them," he said without smiling.

I had been home about half an hour when my mother and Rae came back from the airport. Mother looked displeased, and I hurried to offer my apologies, "I'm really sorry, Mom. I planned on going to the airport with you."

She gave me her no-nonsense look and I knew I was in trouble. "What happened?" she asked.

"We didn't start back in time."

"That's obvious. Chris knew I wanted you home by five. Your brother was disappointed that you didn't care enough to get home in time."

"I'll write to Mac and tell him what happened," I said.

"I think you're seeing too much of Chris. You

have been out with him three nights this week. No more dates on school nights."

"That's not fair! Don't you want me to make friends?"

"Of course I do. But I'd like you to have friends with a sense of responsibility. The world is full of people who can't be counted on," Mother said in an irritated tone.

I couldn't tell my mother we were late because we had fallen asleep in the cabin. She went on sternly, "I'd also like you to concentrate more on your schoolwork."

"My grades are good," I said peevishly. Did she have to treat me like a child?

Rae was reading in bed when I walked by her room. She called me in. "What really happened?" she asked in a low voice.

"We didn't start back in time. That's all there is to it."

"You mean you skied steadily for four hours?"

"Well, we did stop to rest."

She smiled knowingly. "If that's your story, stick to it." The wedding ring quilt was on her bed and the porcelain clock stood on the dresser. "How do you like my room?"

"I see you started the wall mural." Rae had removed the wallpaper and painted the walls a pale apricot, roughing in the mural.

"I'm doing a river scene with the islands and the wildlife."

"No lighthouse?"

"After the crack Chris made about artists and

90

lighthouses? No way! If you're being grounded for a while maybe you'll start doing something about your room. It has the blahs. No character."

Maybe I'd been a fool to give in about the wedding quilt. It would have looked great in my room, too.

CHAPTER
EIGHT

Wonderful things were happening outside. Day by day that week, the land seemed to be rushing toward spring. The sun grew warmer and the snow melted. Rain washed the snow from a corner of the garden. Rae was the first to discover the crocuses—white, orange, and lavender flowers pushing through the wet ground.

We walked around outside, and when my mother discovered something green she would pounce upon it as if it were a long-lost friend. "Grandma's daffodils were along the fence and her herb garden was over there by the back porch—she could just step outside for a sprig of parsley for a roast or chives for a salad. She also grew wintergreen, sweet basil, rosemary, and sage."

She pushed with her foot at the thick, soggy layer of leaves covering the lawn. "We have a lot of cleaning up to do this spring, but it will be worth it to bring Grandma's flowerbeds back to life."

Rae took walks with her sketch pad and came back

with pages full of scenes of the river and the abandoned mill just beyond the bend in the river. I spent hours in the barn foraging among my grandparents' belongings. One day I found a box of pictures, some of them tintypes. That evening my mother went through them and was able to name some of the faces.

"This is my Aunt Doris—she ran a millinery shop in the village in the twenties. She made many of the hats herself. I never knew her, but I heard she was very beautiful and very creative."

"She looks a little like you, Mom," Rae said. "If you put on the fancy hat with feathers, you'd look just like that picture."

"Yes, there is a family resemblance. I just never thought about it." She picked up a picture of a stern-faced man with a mustache, wearing a fireman's uniform. He stood stiff and tall, one hand thrust chest-high into his uniform jacket. "Uncle Theodore lost his life fighting a hotel fire at Alexandria Bay."

"How did that happen?" Rae asked.

"At the turn of the century many big, luxurious hotels were built to accommodate the wealthy who flocked here to enjoy the resort area. Almost all of them were destroyed by fire. The local fire departments didn't have the equipment to save them. My uncle lost his life when a wall collapsed."

Other pictures in the box were identified as baby Eliza who died in the flu epidemic of 1918, cousin Leonard and Eugene who published the town's newspaper in 1925, and Aunt Sarah who ran a boarding house in Clayton. The people in the pictures came alive for me and seemed to surround me with their presence, giving me a feeling of belonging. These were my roots and I wanted to find out more about them.

The highlight of the week was my mother's finding a job. To the relief of Rae and me, she didn't apply for the school-bus driver job but instead answered an ad for help at the museum in the village, which would open for the summer season on the first of May.

"As an old relic myself, I might just get the job," she said as she clipped the ad out of the weekly paper. Antique shops, art galleries, and gift shops were all announcing opening dates. Cory was right. The town did come to life as the weather warmed up.

My mother was ecstatic when she was hired for the museum job. "At least I won't have to compete with young girls. Mrs. DeHaven is at least seventy and she is one smart lady. I'm going to learn a lot about local history from her."

"Maybe I can learn more about our ancestors," I said.

"I'm sure you can. Their newspaper files go back to the 1800s, and they have early census records, too."

"Everyone has a job but me," Rae complained. "I'll probably be stuck doing the housework all summer."

"We'll all share the housework," my mother assured her. "Something may turn up for you, Rae."

"I doubt it," Rae said drearily.

In spite of being grounded on weeknights, things were going well for me at school and I was making friends. Some of the boys who had been to the party made a point of seeking me out. Tom asked me if I was going steady with Chris; when I told him I wasn't, he asked me if I would like to take a ride on his motorcycle after school. It put me on the spot and I put it off, saying I had to do some shopping for my mother.

I wished the boys would pay more attention to Rae. They noticed her all right, but she put on such lofty airs they didn't dare approach her. This was her defense against being hurt, but they didn't know that. She was making girl friends, however. Mariann and she were becoming good friends, painting the stage scenery after school and making plans for the school art show in May. When Rae saw me talking with boys in the hall she pretended not to notice, but I knew her well enough to know she resented it.

As Saturday approached I wondered how my workday would go at the greenhouse. Easter was only two weeks away. Jeffrey had avoided me all week at school and was probably thinking up more tricks to play on me. He didn't know how stubborn I could be; I was determined not to quit.

When I arrived for work, the tulips were a kaleidoscope of color and the Easter lilies were beginning to open. The heady scent of hyacinth and jonquils filled the greenhouse.

Pop Wegman was wrapping the flowerpots in colored foil and attaching ribboned bows. He had a vintage face, tempered by time. His gnarled hands looked out of place among the pink and blue bows.

95

I paused to admire the Easter lilies. "Tell me, how do you get them to bloom just in time for Easter? Easter is a different date every year."

"It's not easy. We had trouble with our heating system one year, and we had two thousand plants that didn't bloom in time. Can you imagine anything harder to sell than an Easter lily after Easter?"

"How about a Christmas tree after Christmas?" I asked.

"Exactly the same problem. Getting them to bloom at the right time is a matter of planting time, temperature control, and feeding."

"What did you do with the two thousand plants?"

"We cut them back and saved the bulbs for next year's planting."

"It must have been a great loss."

Mr. Wegman nodded. "Indeed it was."

Jeffrey came out of the office and walked toward us. "Robin, we're not transplanting today. I'd like you to make some deliveries. Top's Supermarket on Ames Street wants seventy-five Easter plants and Flynn's Market on Clover Street wants sixty combination plants and thirty Easter lilies. When you're through delivering, pick up twenty-five bags of fertilizer at Mason Garden Supply Company in Bergen."

The names meant nothing to me; they might as well have been in a foreign country. "Do you have a map I can use?"

He looked annoyed. "I'll see if I can find one. The delivery van is down by Number 6 greenhouse—you can load the plants from there. Follow me."

I trotted behind him like a pet dog until we

reached Number 6. He indicated the blocks of plants on the benches. "Don't mix up the orders. Here are the invoices, and be sure you have the store managers sign for the deliveries." He handed me the keys to the van. "Load the van so the plants won't tip over if you have to make a sudden stop. Shore up the shelves with planks."

Shore up? What did he mean? Would a boy have known? I started to worry I couldn't do it. The only cars I had ever driven were my mother's. Could I handle a van full of fragile plants? If I had to brake suddenly and the plants went helter-skelter, I'd be fired on the spot.

Jeffrey must have sensed my hesitation. "You can handle the van, can't you?"

"Oh, sure!" I'd bluff my way through. He looked at me suspiciously, not quite believing me. Then he left me to load the one hundred sixty-five plants alone.

I propped the greenhouse door open and backed the van up carefully. The van had a series of shelves to hold the plants. I placed plants on the floor of the van as far as I could reach, and then I climbed up and placed more plants on the shelves. The work went slowly, and I muttered to myself as I climbed in and out of the van. Why didn't Jeffrey send someone to hand the plants up to me? Two people could have loaded the van in fifteen minutes.

I had nearly finished loading when Jeffrey brought me a small map. "We're located here. Ames and Clover Street both run off East Avenue and Bergen is about fifteen miles outside of town on Route 250."

I made a face at him as he turned, and started

back. I still wondered what he meant by "shore up." I remembered boat jargon shore up meant to support with posts or beams. So I found some planks and propped them in such a way that the shelves couldn't slip forward.

I eased the van out of the parking area and onto the road as if I were driving on eggs. Traveling at twenty miles an hour, I located the supermarket and found the manager to ask where he wanted the plants. When he saw I was alone, he sent two boys to help me unload and we carried the plants to display cases in the store.

At Flynn's Market the manager decided to place the plants outside on the sidewalk, since the day was sunny and the colorful display would attract the Easter trade.

I was rather pleased with myself as I headed down Route 250 to the garden supply store. I had delivered the plants without mishap—no boy could have done better. Score one for me. In spite of Jeffrey's macho attitude, I found I liked working around plants. They were living matter, responding to the rhythm of nature. They weren't a dead, manufactured commodity.

I backed the van up to the loading platform and handed my order to one of the employees. Two men worked from a forklift to load the twenty-five bags of fertilizer into the van. I looked at the weight on the bags. One hundred pounds each! Jeffrey expected me to unload the truck?

I bristled with resentment as I drove back. Why was Jeffrey giving me such a hard time? He just didn't want to deal with me, because I was confident of my abilities and I was a girl.

Back at the greenhouse I parked the van, propped open the door and tried to pull out a bag of fertilizer. I couldn't budge it, let alone get a grip on it. Twenty-five bags weighed over a ton, and there was no way I could unload them and get them into the greenhouse by myself.

I'd had it! I was going to tell Jeffrey off! There was no reason for him to treat me this way. All I asked was to be treated fairly. I found Jeffrey on a ladder adjusting the ventilator fan. "Come down here! I want to talk to you!"

He eyed me suspiciously. "What do you want?"

"Just come down here!"

"I'm busy. I can hear you up here." Jeffrey went back to what he was doing."

I rattled the ladder.

"Hey, cut that out. Do you want me to fall?" He climbed down the ladder and stood in front of me. "What's this all about?"

"No way can I unload a ton and a quarter of fertilizer and you know it!"

He smirked. "Then you do admit there are jobs for men and jobs for women."

"The only thing I admit is that where brute strength is required I'm no match for a two-hundred pound man. There are plenty of jobs in here I can do well. You have men in the next greenhouse potting chrysanthemum plants. Why don't you assign me jobs like that?"

"I was watching you. I wouldn't have let you unload the van alone. I just wanted to prove my point," Jeffrey said.

"The heck you did! You wanted me to quit! Well, I won't quit! You can fire me if you want to, but I'm going to your father and tell him he has a jerk for a son."

He cast a worried glance toward the office. "Calm down. I'll send Bill and Henry to unload the van."

"You should have sent them in the first place. I'll bet your father doesn't know about your tricks. He said I wasn't expected to do heavy lifting," I said forcefully.

"It was just a bad joke. Right?"

"Like not telling me to use the high-rise cart last Saturday for the flats?"

"Let's drop the subject. It's time for your lunch break. You can cut some snapdragons for orders to be filled. I can assure you that doesn't call for brute strength. I'll call Pop Wegman to show you how to select the flowers."

I ate my lunch alone outside in the sun. Grace and her friends weren't working today. I still felt trembly over my outburst, and I knew I had antagonized Jeffrey even more. Our personality clash could escalate into an open war, which would make working conditions difficult. And if I looked for another job, it would be conceding to Jeffrey's chauvinism. Some stubborn part of me wasn't ready to settle for that.

Penfield, the gray-and-white cat who patroled for mice and moles in the greenhouse, came over and looked at me expectantly. He must have remembered the piece of tunafish sandwich I had given him last week. "I hope you like cream cheese and olives, Penfield. That's all I have." I broke off some of the sandwich and gave it to him. He ate it daintily, leaving the olives, then disappeared into the weeds, and I was alone again.

After lunch, I moved about cutting pink, yellow, and white snapdragons, wrapping them by the dozen in green waxed paper. Mr. Neuman stopped by. "Robin, could you help us out tomorrow? Marcia, the girl who clerks in our retail store, can't come tomorrow, and Mrs. Neuman and I have to attend a funeral out of town. I'd appreciate it if you could work. I realize it's Sunday and you may have other plans."

"Do you think I could handle the store? I've never clerked before."

"I'm sure you could. The prices are all marked, and Marcia will show you now how to operate the cash register," Mr. Neuman explained.

"Yes, I can work. What time should I be here?"

"The store hours are from ten A.M. to five P.M. on Sundays. With Easter so close, you may be busy taking orders. Come with me and I'll introduce you to Marcia."

I felt a little apprehensive as I followed Mr. Neuman. The thought of operating the cash register was scary. Suppose I handed out the wrong change if it got too busy for me to handle alone?

The store was decorated for Easter with yellow and purple displays. Ceramic rabbits and chickens filled with floral arrangements were everywhere. A glass-fronted cooler was filled with cut flowers— roses, carnations, and orchid corsages.

101

Mr. Neuman left me with Marcia. She was twenty and excited about her upcoming marriage in June. As she showed me around the store, she went into great detail about her wedding plans, the showers her girl friends were giving her, and what her future husband was like. Through her chatter, I tried to keep straight how to figure the sales tax, take down phone orders, and charge for deliveries. I was afraid all I'd remember was that Marcia's wedding gown had a Queen Anne neckline and the reception for two hundred fifty guests would be held at Stoltz Party House.

"I have to work tomorrow," I told my mother when I came home.

"On Sunday?"

"I'm helping out. Mr. Neuman needs someone in the store."

Rae was cutting out a blouse on the kitchen table. She looked up. "A Jeffrey Neuman is helping to direct the musical at school. Is there any connection?"

"Sure thing. He's Mr. Neuman's only son and heir."

"What a great-looking guy! Mariann has a crush on him, but he doesn't even know she exists," Rae said.

"Well, his personality isn't so great. I prefer the company of Penfield, the greenhouse cat."

"Come on, Robin, He can't be that bad. Mariann would work at Neuman's for free if they'd hire her."

"Mariann sounds a little flaky." Rae looked annoyed, and I walked into my room to rest before dinner.

Chris called after supper. "Hi, how did work go today?"

"All right. I have to work tomorrow."

"On Sunday?" Chris asked.

"That's exactly what my mother said."

"Now I *am* jealous."

"Chris, if only you knew how ridiculous that sounds. Jeffrey thinks I founded women's lib," I said sarcastically.

"Can I pick you up after work? We could go into Watertown for a movie."

"I don't know if I can go out on a school night. Why don't you come over for supper instead?"

"Your mother's not mad at me anymore?"

"No, and anyway, you both should get better acquainted since you and I are friends."

"To know me is to love me," Chris joked.

"Conceit will get you nowhere—with my mother *or* me. So watch it."

"I love you," he said softly as he hung up the phone.

CHAPTER
NINE

Charcoal gray clouds hovered menacingly in the sky as I unlocked the store on Sunday morning. The wind had propelled me down the road as I walked to work, whipping my hair about my face and stinging my cheeks. The air had grown colder, and ice lace was beginning to form on the edges of the puddles along the road.

Inside, I moved about the store, turning on the lights, checking the money in the cash register, making sure I had an order pad and pencil next to the phone. I felt good being in charge of the store.

Mr. Neuman stopped in briefly before he and his wife left for the funeral. "If you have any questions, Robin, or if some problem should arise, get in touch with Jeffrey. None of the men will be working today, but Jeffrey is looking after the place while we're gone."

He went to the window and looked out. "The weather station reported that high winds are expected throughout the day. Our greenhouses are vulnerable in storms. I'm uneasy about being away today but we promised we'd go." As they waved good-bye, the wind rattled the windows of the store as if trying to get in, and the sign mounted outside on a post swung crazily back and forth.

The morning passed quickly. Families stopped in to order plants to be sent to grandparents in time for Easter. Floral arrangements were ordered to decorate holiday tables. I realized for the first time what part flowers play in the important events in our lives—birthdays, weddings, anniversaries, funerals, sickness, holidays.

The customers complained about the high winds and said the temperature had dropped twenty degrees in a few hours. The sky pressed down like a smothering curtain. My mother phoned later in the day. "Are you all right, Robin? A storm alert has been broadcast."

"I'm fine, Mom. Don't worry."

"I don't like to think of you being there alone."

"I'll be all right. If it's storming at closing time I'll call Chris to pick me up. He won't mind. He's coming for supper."

Jeffrey had not come near the store, but I had seen him at a distance going in and out of the greenhouses. I hoped I wouldn't have to call on him for help today. When the rain began to fall, it was in wind-driven sheets, the wind rising to a ghastly wail. The world turned dark, and the wind and rain made so much noise I became frightened. I had never been alone in a violent storm before.

The lights flickered a few times then went out.

Trash cans rolled and tumbled along the driveway; tree branches and debris flew through the air. I thought I heard the sound of breaking glass.

I peered out the window and could see Jeffrey running toward the store. I knew something was wrong. As I opened the door, the wind caught it and nearly tore it from its hinges. Jeffrey dashed in. His cheek was cut and bleeding, and he was soaking wet. "I've got to get help! The wind broke up the old shed in back and sent it crashing into Number 6 greenhouse!" He picked up the phone.

The Easter plants were in Number 6 greenhouse! The rain and the wind would ruin them if the glass was smashed. Maybe I could save some of them. I grabbed my jacket and raced through the connecting tunnel from the store to the greenhouse.

When I reached Number 6 I saw the great jagged opening in the roof and the rain pouring down over the flowers. Glass lay everywhere, most of it embedded in the plants, and the wind screamed through the opening, whipping the flowers. The Easter lilies were overturned and lay in pools of muddy water.

I located a cart and began loading the plants I thought could be saved. It was disheartening. I had to discard many of them that had been shredded by the glass. When the cart was full I wheeled it to a safe location down the aisle and unloaded them.

When I went back for a second load, Jeffrey came running up. "The phones are dead and I couldn't reach any of the men. The heat is off and it's near freezing outside. If I don't get some canvas over that opening we'll lose all the plants in here."

"I'll help you," I offered.

He looked at me as if I were out of my mind. "What help could you be?"

"I could hold the canvas while you secure it."

"It's too dangerous for a girl. You could crash through the glass."

"Let me try," I insisted.

He didn't answer me, but I followed him into a storeroom where he located a long roll of canvas. "You stay here until I come back for the ladders," he ordered. "See if you can find a pair of gloves. I don't want you cutting your hands."

I located a pair of work gloves and waited by the door. The wind seemed to have subsided a bit and the rain had settled into a steady downpour. Jeffrey came back and located three aluminum ladders. He handed me the shortest one. I followed him through the rain to Number 6.

The glass roof rose about thirty feet to a peak. "How can you climb on the glass? Won't you fall through?"

"I know where to climb. Certain sections are reinforced." He placed the short ladder against the wall of the greenhouse and the two longer ladders about fifteen feet apart on the roof. Then he started to climb up with the roll of canvas.

"Robin, inch your way up the ladder and try to hold on to your end of the canvas. Lie on it if you can't hold it down."

I climbed the short ladder to reach the roof and looked down through the glass. Would the roof really hold me or would I go crashing through to the broken glass below? I moved onto the long ladder laying flat against the glass roof. Like a movie in slow motion, I crept upward, my stomach hugging the rungs of the ladder.

"I hope you're not afraid of heights," Jeffrey shouted. He was securing his end of the canvas with metal hooks.

The wind billowed the canvas and I fought to hold it. My father and I had been out in the bay with our sailboat once when we were caught in a storm and our sail ripped. I remembered how we had struggled with the sail. That's the way it was now, as the wind tore the canvas from my hands. Finally I got hold of a corner of it and held it down with my body.

Long minutes passed as I huddled there, not daring to move. The rain beat down on me, soaking my hair, running down my neck. Then Jeffrey was on the ladder beside me. "It's all right, Robin. You can go back down. I'll take over now."

Back on the ground I stood shaking from the cold and rain as I watched Jeffrey anchor down my side of the canvas. I breathed a long sigh of relief.

He climbed down the ladder. "I think it will hold now, and it will keep out most of the cold and the rain. We'll put a crew to work replacing the glass tomorrow. You're soaking wet. Come in the house and I'll find you some dry clothes."

"Can't you just take me home?"

"In those wet clothes? You'll get pneumonia," Jeffrey said.

"I'll be all right. Your face is cut. Let me take care of it."

"It's nothing."

"It should be cleaned off. Where's your first-aid kit?" I insisted.

"In the office, but you don't have to bother."

"Come on. I'm taking charge now." I found the first-aid kit and I made Jeffrey sit on a stool while I washed the cut. It wasn't deep, and I didn't think it would need stitches.

"You may have an interesting scar, the kind you might get from a sword flick in a duel," I commented as I applied antiseptic.

He turned and faced me. "Robin, I owe you all kinds of apologies. I've been obnoxious and I'm really sorry. No guy could have done more than you did today."

I packed the bandages and antiseptic back in the kit. "Then I proved a point, too."

"The day you came here looking for a job you acted sort of wise and I thought, here's that girl from California who's laughing at me. She thinks I'm from this hick town and don't know what it's all about."

"First impressions can be wrong."

"Then at Monty's you showed off and made that crack about livening up the party. I wanted to cut you down, but I was wrong about you. You didn't have to risk your neck up on that roof today. I guess I've never met a girl like you," Jeffrey said.

"Maybe we were both wrong about each other."

"Give me another chance. Why don't we pretend we've just met and forget all that happened? Are you willing to do that?"

"All right. I'm not hard to get along with. Are the plants going to be okay?" I asked.

"If the power is off for any length of time, I can put kerosene heaters in the greenhouse to take off the chill. The important thing was getting the hole covered. If the temperature dropped below thirty-two degrees we could have lost everything in there."

"What should I do about the store?"

"It's nearly four o'clock—I'm sure we won't have any customers in this weather. Let's lock up and you can come in the house and get some dry clothes."

"Why don't you just take me home, Jeffrey? My mother is probably worried about me."

"If you say so, Robin. I'll drive over to Bill's, and if he's home he can come over and help me clean up the glass."

As we drove, we saw that many trees had been uprooted. In one place we had to drive around a heavy limb that had fallen across the road. "Do you think it was a tornado?" I asked.

"No, it could have been a line storm. That's a narrow band of strong winds that can cause heavy damage, but they don't have the force of a tornado," Jeffrey explained.

"I hope I'm never in a tornado. This storm was scary enough."

"Thanks again, Robin," he said as he let me out in our driveway. "I'll see you in school tomorrow?" How could anyone who had acted so miserably turn out to be so likable? When he turned on the charm, wow!

My mother was relieved when I arrived home safely. "I tried calling you but the phones are out of order. Rae's little transistor radio was the only way of finding out what was happening. When I heard about all the storm damage, I was worried."

"I'm glad you didn't know I was on the greenhouse roof trying to hold down a twenty-foot piece of canvas."

My mother looked horrified. "What were they thinking of, sending you up on the roof in the storm?"

"I volunteered."

"Never volunteer," Rae said. "I learned that in an army movie. Was that Jeff Neuman who brought you home?"

"The one and only," I answered.

"Were you up on the roof with him?"

"Unfortunately."

"I know lots of girls who would risk life and limb to go up on the roof with him."

"Rae, I think you like Jeffrey."

"He's got class—I will say that for him. When he's a famous director someday, you can say you worked for him."

My mother was indignant. "This is nothing to joke about, girls. I can't understand the Neumans endangering Robin's life."

"It was an emergency, Mom. The storm blew the glass out, and Jeffrey and I were the only ones there."

"You're soaking wet, too. Get in the tub and take a hot bath."

"Chris will be coming soon. What are we having for supper?"

"I made spaghetti and meat balls. Rae made some

garlic bread and a tossed salad. I'm glad the power came back on, or we'd be eating cold sandwiches," Mother said.

"I don't think Chris is fussy," I replied. "I don't know what I base my opinion on—I'm just assuming he isn't hard to please."

Chris arrived about six o'clock. "Did the marina suffer any storm damage?" my mother asked.

"Our big sign blew down, but that's about all. If the storm had come later in the year when the boats are docked, it would have been a disaster."

I took his jacket and put it on a hanger. "Did you hear what happened at Neuman's?"

"My father heard about it on the CB radio. How much damage did it do?"

"We lost several hundred plants and about a hundred and fifty panes of glass," I told him.

"We would have lost Robin, too, if she had fallen through the roof," Rae offered.

Chris frowned. "You were on the roof?"

"Please, nothing happened. We did what we had to do. It was no big deal. How is supper coming, Mom?"

"We're ready to eat. Robin, drain the spaghetti, and Rae, take the garlic bread out of the oven."

After supper we all watched TV and played a few games of cards. We had a good time. Rae was actually pleasant, and I was glad she and Chris had decided to become friends.

"Chris isn't so bad when you get to know him," she said as she was getting ready for bed.

"I've been trying to tell you that, Rae. You never

gave him a chance to know you. You just came on like the Witch of the West."

She shrugged her shoulders and gave me a half-smile. Was my sister becoming interested in boys? If only she would shed her defensive attitude around them.

"Most boys are just as unsure of themselves as girls are," I said. "Sometimes they need a little encouragement."

Rae picked up her hairbrush and began brushing her hair. "Is this your instant psychology lesson for today?" she asked sarcastically.

"No, just stating the facts of life," I answered calmly.

"You're very boring when you get on this subject, Robin. I notice you didn't snarl today when you mentioned Jeffrey's name. What does that mean?"

"It means I might have changed my mind about him."

"Where does that leave Chris?"

"He's still in first place. I'm going to bed now. I'll see you in the morning." I cut her off and walked into my own room.

CHAPTER
TEN

The next morning I was in the library doing research for a composition for English class. We had a choice of topics and I chose "Superstition" because it sounded interesting and a little weird. Titles like "Polarization of Light" and "Medicine in the Fifteenth Century" were unlikely choices, especially since Mr. Colburn said he wanted twenty-five hundred words on the subject.

I hadn't expected the research to be so interesting. Exploring the origins of different superstitions—like walking under a ladder, or opening an umbrella indoors—was really interesting. I was engrossed in a book when Jeffrey came by.

"Hi, Robin. What do you find so interesting?" Jeffrey put his books on the library table and sat down beside me.

"Did you know a wolf's tooth worn on a chain prevents nightmares?"

"You must have picked 'Superstition' for your English theme. I picked 'The History of the Theater' and I haven't even started working on it yet."

"It's due Thursday."

He smiled. "If you're going to be here all period, I'll start on it right now. Are you any the worse for your experience yesterday?"

"A hot bath slowly brought my temperature back to ninety-eight degrees."

"Not even a sore throat?"

"I'm incredibly healthy. By the way, have you met my sister Rae yet? She's a fan of yours. She's sure you're going to be a famous director someday."

"I met Rae. She's helping with the scenery. You don't look like sisters."

"Rae's the pretty one—that's how my relatives refer to her."

"Come on! The guys all noticed you, but Chris moved in too fast. He has the advantage of being your nearest neighbor. How serious is it with you two?"

"We're friends. Now let's get back to you. Are you choosing the theater for a career?" I said.

"Definitely, but I'm planning on going to college, too, and getting all the experience I can in college and little theater groups."

"Doesn't your dad want you to continue in the florist business?"

"Naturally he'd like me to carry on the business, but he feels he's been happy in his work and he wants to give me the chance to live my own life," Jeffrey confided.

"Your dad's a neat guy. Not all fathers feel that way. Anyway, the librarian is glaring at us. We'd better get down to work before she throws us out."

"She's just bluffing. My dad was impressed when I

told him how you helped me on the roof. I'm supposed to ask you if you can work Wednesday afternoon in the greenhouse and Easter vacation in the store. Marcia is busy with wedding plans and wants the week off. Did you know she's getting married?"

"I know all about her wedding plans. Also the fact that her future husband is extremely possessive and her future mother-in-law doesn't want them to have children for two years."

He laughed. "Marcia doesn't keep any secrets."

"I'll be glad to work," I said.

"Good. I'll pick you up after school Wednesday. Okay?"

I agreed but I felt apprehensive. Chris was beginning to send out signals of jealousy over Jeffrey and I didn't think he'd like my riding with him. I hoped I'd made it clear to Chris I wanted to be my own person. I didn't know if he was mature enough to accept the fact that I liked him but could still be on friendly terms with other boys, too.

Tuesday afternoon Rae stayed after school to work on the scenery. When I came in the house my mother handed me a letter without speaking. It was from my father, and it contained two plane tickets and an invitation for Rae and me to visit him and his new wife in Chicago during our summer vacation. "I obtained the tickets early," he wrote, "to take advantage of special rates and give you girls time to make plans. I'd like you to spend the whole summer, if you want to. Excellent art courses are offered at the university which I know will interest you, Rae, and Robin, there are endless opportunities here for

116

volunteer work with youth agencies, which will be helpful in your career. The enclosed brochures will explain the art courses and the youth agencies that use volunteers."

I glanced at my mother, who had busied herself at the sink chopping celery for a casserole. "He has a lot of nerve. Does he really think I'd leave you alone?"

"Your father has every right to ask you," she replied.

"He knows what he can do with the tickets."

"He's still your father."

"When he moved out of the house he stopped being my father!"

"Rae may feel differently. I know she misses him."

"Well, I don't miss him!" It wasn't exactly true, but I wanted Mom to know I felt loyal to her.

Rae did feel differently when she came home and read the letter. "Oh, Mom! Can we go? Imagine taking classes at the university!"

"Count me out," I answered.

My mother said. "I don't think Robin is interested, Rae, but you're free to go."

"I couldn't go without Robin. I've never traveled alone."

"I'll be working this summer," I said.

"Would you really let your job prevent you from going with me? Or is it Chris?"

"I wouldn't leave Mom alone. Besides, I'm not interested in spending the summer in Chicago."

"You're being selfish, Robin. Say you'll go with me! Please! You don't mind if we go, do you, Mom?"

"Your father can ask you to spend vacations with him. It was part of the divorce settlement."

"See, Mom doesn't care!" Rae exclaimed.

"I could get Aunt Martha to come and stay with me if you girls want to go," my mother answered. "I don't want to stand in your way."

My mother is as bad as I am, I thought. We'll feel guilty about denying Rae a chance to study art this summer and we'll give in to her.

Rae leafed through the brochures. "Look at this! There are classes in New Image art, sculpture, charcoal drawing, ornamental art, and portrait! You've got to come with me, Robin! You'll change your mind, just you wait and see!"

Jeffrey picked me up after school Wednesday afternoon to drive me to work. I hoped Chris didn't see me get in Jeffrey's car, but I was sure that if he didn't someone would tell him about it.

"I have an easy job for you today. You'll be potting Swedish ivy and Boston fern in hanging baskets."

"I don't expect any special consideration. I just don't intend to unload hundred-pound bags of fertilizer."

"I've already apologized for that. We were going to forget it, remember?" He glanced at his watch. "We have twenty minutes before you start work. I'd like to show you something I've been working on."

"A new hybrid strain of petunias?"

"No, something more interesting than that." He parked in the driveway and I followed him into a long, low building adjacent to the greenhouses. He flicked on an overhead fluorescent light, and there

118

was a beautiful launch, its mahogany hull gleaming softly. The cabin roof had scalloped edges, like a surrey, and the seats were dark red leather. Gold letters formed the word *Algonquin* on the hull.

"It's beautiful!" I exclaimed.

"I've been restoring it for two years. My father bought it at a boat auction a few years ago. It belonged to the old Crossman Hotel that burned down. It was used as a tour boat for the guests."

I trailed my hand along the polished brass rail. "Is it seaworthy?"

"I'm taking it on a trial run during Easter vacation. The engine seems in good condition, and I'd like to enter it in the Antique Boat Regatta in August. It's quite an event—it attracts boating enthusiasts from all over the country."

"My dad had a sailboat and we were out on the bay almost every weekend."

"You're a good sailor then? Would you like to go on the trial run with me?"

"Sounds great. I hope I can be useful as a crew member."

"I'll take that chance." Jeffrey seemed so confident, so sure of what he wanted and how to go after it.

We left the building and went into Number 3 greenhouse, where he gave me instructions for my afternoon's work. I worked all afternoon potting the hanging plants in their white plastic containers. As I finished each one I hung it on a wire strung between two poles in the greenhouse.

Mr. Neuman stopped by. "You have a nice touch with plants, Robin."

"I like working in the earth with living things. I hate artificial plants and flowers."

"The earth has music for those who listen," he answered.

"I believe that. If I didn't have plans for a career in political science, I might consider horticulture."

"Why not consider it as a relaxing hobby?"

"My own greenhouse? I'd like that," I said.

"Would you consider working full-time in the store this summer? Marcia gave us notice she'll be leaving in June after her wedding."

A full-time job! Great! I could save money to help with my college expenses. "I'd love the job!"

"It will take training. We'll teach you to make corsages as well as floral arrangements. Your advice will be asked about flowers for weddings and special occasions," Mr. Neuman explained.

I must have looked blank because he smiled. "We'll teach you, of course. Trends change in flowers as well as fashions."

I felt rather pleased with myself when Mr. Neuman left. I was carving a niche for myself in this north country community.

CHAPTER
ELEVEN

The weather turned warm again. Pale sheaves of daffodils and iris shoots shone beneath the brown wreckage of last year's flowers. The ice was entirely gone from the river now, and I watched the gulls soaring over the water, floating patches of white against the sky. They rode the wavelets for hours, then rose gently into the air. The forsythia bushes were a sunny glow against the house, and I gathered pussy willows and put them in a blue enameled coffeepot I found in the barn.

My mother, Rae, and I raked the lawn after school and put the dead leaves in bushel crates along the road to be picked up by the refuse trucks. We prowled about in the barn and gradually replaced some of our furniture with the heirloom pieces stored there.

We decided Grandma's marble-topped parlor table would look elegant in the living room, and the cherry schoolmaster's desk replaced a modern lamp table. I loved cleaning and polishing the old wood to bring back its mellow glow.

We gave up on the chicken house as a studio for Rae. The floor had rotted away and most of the windows were broken. "It's an eyesore," my mother decided, "and should be torn down. Maybe Mac could build you a little place out there."

"He'll never have time," Rae grumbled. "I'll be old and decrepit before he gets around to it."

"We may find a local carpenter who works reasonably. I don't think it would cost too much to build a room."

"You have the whole outdoors to paint in this summer," I offered.

"Where do you expect me to keep my canvases, my paints, my brushes? In my dresser drawer with my underwear?"

"We'll work out something," my mother said soothingly. "Maybe we could sell some of the things in the barn and raise a little money."

I looked up quickly to see if my mother was joking. She wasn't. She was dead serious. I could think of other things more important than a studio for Rae. We needed a new roof on the house; in heavy rains brown stains appeared on the bedroom ceilings. The ancient bathroom fixtures were ready to give up. My mother and I were caught in a web of self-sacrifice for Rae.

We were putting the last of the leaves out by the road when Chris drove up. He leaned out the window. "I got my boat out today. Would you all like to go for a ride?"

"Thanks, Chris, but I have bread ready to go in the oven. Maybe some other time," my mother answered.

"I have to start my homework or I'd go along," Rae replied.

He looked disappointed. I knew he had been looking forward to taking us out in his boat. "There's nothing to stop me," I answered with enthusiasm. Then I paused. "I forgot. I'm grounded."

"You're grounded school nights," my mother said. "Can I expect you home in time for supper?"

"I'll have her here by five, Mrs. Thomas. I'm sorry about Sunday night. It was poor planning on my part."

My mother had her no-nonsense look. "I don't mean to be unfair. I'm trying to impress Robin with the importance of keeping her word."

I felt embarrassed. She sounded like a cliché mother in a high school play. Chris looked subdued. "We'll be back in time."

We got in the car and headed toward the marina. "Whew! I'm always getting in trouble with your mother. Is she that hard on all your boyfriends?"

"What do you mean—all my boyfriends?"

"How about that Kevin character back in California?"

"We're just friends. He's going to Alaska this summer."

"Not to stay?"

"He'll be back to start his senior year. I'm being realistic. Of course Kevin will be dating other girls."

"You don't seem bent out of shape over it."

"I'm sure he expects I'll be dating, too. I had planned on going back home this summer as sort of a Band-Aid in keeping our relationship together. That was before I knew he was going to Alaska," I explained.

"We'll all be going our separate ways after graduation next year. It seems sort of sad when you think about it."

Boats bobbed in the water along the pier, and the waves slapped like bare hands at the pilings. Far away a coal barge moved upriver toward the Seaway. Chris parked in the lot behind the marina and, holding hands, we walked out on the pier.

He said with a shy grin, "When I was a little boy, I used to think the river talked to me. It seemed to say 'Hurry up! Hurry up!' as it made its way toward the ocean."

I smiled. "I wish I had known you as a little boy."

"I was a rotten little kid. My sister used to call me 'The Mouth.' Would you like to meet my mother? She's getting the store ready. We're opening on Saturday for the season."

Mrs. Taber, a pleasant-faced woman in jeans and a sweat shirt, was stocking the shelves with boating supplies. "I've been meaning to get over and meet your mother. We've talked on the phone."

"She'll be glad to meet you. We really appreciated all you did for us the night we moved in."

"Now that winter is over, perhaps we can get together. Have you met Amy?"

Amy was a grasshopper-thin little blonde about ten years old. "I'm going to work in the store this summer," she announced. "I'm learning to make change."

"We'll probably go bankrupt," Chris added. "Math isn't Amy's best subject."

"Don't tease her," his mother replied. "She's doing quite well."

Amy stuck her tongue out at Chris. "Dad didn't let you make change until you were thirteen. So there!"

"Lovely child," Chris commented. "Let's hit the water, Robin."

"I've been wanting to explore the islands," I said to Mrs. Taber. "Some of them look so mysterious."

"The majority of the islands are privately owned and you could get arrested for trespassing. But Chris knows a few that are abandoned."

I said good-bye, and Chris and I cast off in a speedboat as sleek as a barracuda in the blue, sparkling water. I loved the feel of the wind in my hair and against my face. We passed the luxurious homes on the islands, where I could see workmen preparing the lawns and working about the boathouses.

A few miles out, Chris cut the motor and we drifted toward an island. In the midst of grounds overgrown with underbrush stood the remains of a fortresslike mansion, whose vacant windows stared back like the eyes of the mindless dead. Crumbling stone towers rose above the stone walls, and at the water's edge the ruins of a boathouse sloped into the water.

Chris tied the boat to the rotted remains of an old pier. "You can explore here to your heart's content. This was all built around 1890 by an oil baron, Wilfried Heinrich, and destroyed by fire in 1940."

"We won't be trespassing?"

"No, it's been abandoned for some time. There's nothing left of value. Only the shell of the residence

125

and the boathouse remain. At the turn of the century millionaires docked their yachts in the boathouse, and Heinrich was so wealthy he staged treasure hunts at his parties with real jewelry hidden on the grounds."

"Wow! Do you suppose some of it is still hidden here?"

"People have been searching for years with metal detectors, but I haven't heard of anyone finding anything valuable. Maybe a key or brass fixtures but no diamond necklaces."

We walked through the remains of a formal garden and past a circular pool stagnant and coated with dead leaves. A flock of redwinged blackbirds scattered before us. The massive door creaked on its hinges like the sound effects of a horror movie as we entered a vast space that must have been a ballroom. A shattered chandelier lay where it had fallen from the ceiling, and charred furniture was strewn about.

The desolation saddened me. "Think about the parties and the dances this room has seen."

"How about the intrigue, the secret love affairs, the skeletons in the closets?"

"I always wanted to be a skeleton in somebody's closet," I mused.

"You're weird, Robin." Chris took me in his arms. "Let's go back in time. May I have this waltz, my love?"

We danced around the ballroom. We were both laughing now and we nearly tripped over some rubbish. "I wonder if there are any bats in here?" Chris asked casually. "Don't they go with haunted houses?"

"Bats!" I screamed, conjuring a picture of the evil-faced little creatures tangling in my hair. "Haunted! I'm getting out of here!"

"We've only begun to explore the house. Don't you want to climb up in the tower?"

"I'll do my exploring outside!"

"Of course, we may have to contend with snakes sunning themselves on the rocks."

I was appalled. Gooseflesh fanned out over my body. Snakes were even worse than bats! "Chris!"

"Where's your sense of adventure? Don't you want to hunt for hidden jewelry?" Chris asked.

"After that remark about the snakes? No thanks!"

"I was only teasing."

"Is the place really haunted?" I asked.

"Some people say that just before a storm old Heinrich roams about the place with a lantern. They swear they can see the light from shore."

"Do you believe it?"

"I think people want to believe it's haunted."

"Maybe we shouldn't be here. It might bring us bad luck."

"Come on, Robin. The dead won't hurt you. It's the living you have to watch out for."

We sat down on the stone terrace and watched a grey heron standing motionless on the rocks waiting for an unwary fish. "Is it true they swim under water and pull down baby ducks for food?" I asked.

Chris nodded. "Nature's law of survival."

"They look so aloof and regal and they're nothing but bandits."

Chris reached out and mussed my hair. "I wasn't

going to tell you until next week, but I have a surprise for you." He looked pleased with himself.

"What is it?"

"Have you heard about the rock concert a week from Saturday at Cape Vincent? It's an all-day affair."

"I've heard the kids talking about it. I can't believe all the great rock groups are coming here."

"I bought two tickets for us," Chris said.

"Oh, Chris, I'll be working in the store!"

"Tell Mr. Neuman to get someone else to work that Saturday."

"I can't do that, Chris. I've just started working there," I said.

He frowned. "I paid twelve-fifty for the tickets."

"I'm really sorry. If I'd known sooner you were buying tickets I wouldn't have told Mr. Neuman I'd work. I could meet you at the concert after work."

There was a stubborn set to his mouth. "I want to spend the day there and I wanted to spend it with you."

"I feel terrible about this, Chris. Look, if you want someone to go with, why don't you ask Rae? She'd love to go."

"Rae! She can't stand me!"

"She likes you. She just doesn't know how to act around boys."

"Someone should show her!" Chris said angrily.

"Rae has never had a date. It would mean a lot to her."

"I don't want to go with your sister. I want to go with you! It's Jeff Neuman, isn't it? That's why you

128

want to put your sister off on me. You'd rather spend the day working with Jeff!"

"Don't be ridiculous, Chris! Please try to understand. I like my job and I want to keep it. I want to show Mr. Neuman I'm reliable. He's asked me to work full-time in the store this summer."

"Just come out and tell me if you don't want to go with me anymore. I saw you and Jeff in the library together."

I felt the tears welling up in my eyes. "Chris, I'd rather be with you than any boy I know."

"I may not be cool or a big shot in school, but I love you, Robin. I thought what we felt for each other was the real thing, but I guess the caring was all on my side."

I faced him almost pleadingly. "That's not true."

"Maybe you've decided to write me off as casually as you did Kevin."

I knew Chris was quick-tempered and had shown signs of being jealous of Jeff, but I thought he'd understand about my job. I had mentioned Rae because it would give her a chance to get out and have some fun, and this would also ease my guilty feelings. I tried to hold back the tears. "Maybe you're not that special person I thought you were. If there is one thing I can't stand it's jealousy."

"Then we're both disappointed, Robin, and perhaps it's best we break up before we hurt each other any more." The words fell like blows.

I was shocked and hurt. My usual reaction when my feelings were hurt was to strike back, to say something devastating, but now I felt too numbed to respond.

"We'd better get back," he said brusquely. "I have a lot to do before dark."

There was nothing to do but follow him down to the boat. I sat very still while he untied the boat and started the motor. Chris will get over this and call me, I thought. Hadn't he explained how he often spoke without thinking and got over it just as quickly? He'll call me as if nothing happened.

But he didn't call. He passed me in school the next day with just a nod. The day dragged by, trailing suspense behind it as I waited for him to make some sign we could be friends again. I was too proud to make the first move.

At noon, in the cafeteria, I ate with the girls instead of with Chris at our special table in the back of the room. I tried to concentrate on my studies but all I could think about was Chris—how special he made me feel, the fun we had together.

In English class we were studying poetry. Miss Winters asked me to read aloud "A Walk on the Beach" by John Gould Fletcher, and my voice trembled so much I could hardly read. Cory turned around in her seat and looked at me. I felt she suspected something was wrong but didn't want to ask.

At home I expected someone would observe the fact Chris wasn't phoning me in the evening for our hour-long conversations, but neither Rae or my mother seemed to notice. My mother was busy making preparations for Easter; she had invited Uncle Bob and Aunt Helen to spend the holiday with us. More and more things from the barn were replacing our California furniture, and she wanted our house in the best possible condition. Rae was working on an art project and spent all her time in her room.

We got out of school the Thursday before Easter to start our vacation. When we got off the school bus Rae said, "I didn't want to say anything on the bus, but are you and Chris having trouble?"

I tried to sound casual. "Why?"

"A strange thing happened today. Chris asked me if I'd like to go to the rock festival with him next week."

I couldn't look at her. I brushed some lint from the sleeve of my sweater. "What did you tell him?"

"I said I'd think about it."

"You should have accepted." The hurt pushed at me even though I tried to smile.

Her face was a watchful mask. "Have you broken up with him? I want to be sure. I wouldn't make trouble between you."

"There's nothing between us anymore."

"You have to be kidding!" Rae said.

"Have you heard him call lately? Have you seen him hanging around?"

"No . . . but you seemed so right together."

"Only on the surface. Chris has some growing up to do," I said.

"Do you want to talk about it?"

"No."

"I wonder why he asked *me?* There are plenty of other girls he could have asked."

"He's always liked you but you were too dumb to notice."

"Maybe he feels sorry for me."

131

"Boys don't ask girls out because they feel sorry for them."

"I wish I was sure," Rae said.

"Why analyze his offer? Just go and have a good time." Even as I said it I hoped my voice didn't sound strained and twisted. I had asked Chris to take Rae to the concert, but I hadn't expected it would be under these circumstances.

"I don't know what to wear or what to say!" A hint of panic crept into her voice. "Robin, I've never been on a date before."

"There's a first time for everyone." All my life I had wanted the best for Rae, to see her happy and enjoying life like other teenagers. But did it have to be with Chris? Why did I tell him to invite her? I was only hurting myself.

From that moment everything changed. The fuss about Rae's coming date consumed our waking hours. Her moods swung from uncertainty to vivacity to dejection. She was sure she would be such a dull date he would never ask her out again.

Finally, in exasperation, my mother took her arm and marched her over to a mirror. "That's why he asked you out, Rae. For heaven's sake, relax!" My mother seemed pleased Chris had asked Rae to the concert, and I guess she just took it for granted that Chris and I had a very casual relationship.

I was glad to leave it that way. I'd study harder and think about college. I would keep so busy I'd forget all about Chris. Deep inside I knew I was just kidding myself.

CHAPTER
TWELVE

On Easter Sunday Chris called as we were finishing dinner. When Rae came back to the phone she was glowing. "Is it all right if I go for a boat ride with Chris? He wants to take me to Boldt Castle. It's a replica of an old German castle."

My mother hesitated. "We do have guests, Rae."

"I want to see it, Mother. I may want to do some sketches there during vacation."

"Let her go," Uncle Bob said. "Everyone has to visit Boldt Castle at least once."

"It's only a tourist trap," I answered. "Commercialism at its worst." What was wrong with me? I sounded as bitter as Rae used to be when I was leaving on a date and she was left at home.

Uncle Bob replied, "It's one of our biggest attractions and its chief fascination lies in the fact it was never completed. Millionaire George Boldt was building it as a Valentine's Day gift for his wife, and when she died in 1902 he ordered the work stopped. He never returned to the island. Vandals took everything of value and desecrated the place."

"It's a bittersweet love story—it always fascinated me as a girl," Aunt Helen said. "How romantic to see it with your young man, Rae."

I remembered the wintry day Chris had promised to take me to Boldt Castle as soon as the ice broke on the river. I wasn't used to being left behind, and it hurt. I helped with the dishes and later went for a walk in the fields. I felt restless and lonely and very sorry for myself.

I had no one to talk to. Maybe Mac, if he was here, would listen to me. I knew what he'd say. "If you want Chris so badly, swallow your pride and try to get him back." It wasn't that easy. I couldn't compete with my sister who was handicapped. It wasn't fair.

Later in the day Rae called to say that Chris had taken her to meet his parents and she was staying for supper.

"It looks as if our little Rae has gotten herself a boyfriend," my mother said as she hung up the phone. Aunt Helen and Uncle Bob had left and we were alone.

I was noncommittal. "Could be."

"This could do so much for Rae. If you only knew how my heart aches for her, sitting home by herself week after week."

I didn't answer.

"Have you thought any more about visiting your father this summer, Robin?"

"What would I do in Chicago all summer, Mother? Visit the stockyards?" I said bitterly.

"It would mean so much to Rae. Art is her life."

I have my dreams, too, I thought. Don't you care about mine?

"If you don't want to go for the whole summer, perhaps just go for six weeks so she could take one of the courses."

"Mom, I told you how I feel."

"Think it over carefully. I should contact Aunt Martha if there is a chance you might go."

I sighed. I felt as if a net were being thrown over my head and tightened. I was in bed when Rae came in and I pretended to be asleep. I didn't want to talk to her and hear about what happened today. But I wasn't so lucky.

She gave me a shake. "Robin! Wake up! I had the best time! We went all through the castle and even climbed up in the turret where Chris wrote our names on the wall. It was all filled with hundreds of names Chris said had been there for ages, and when we're old we can come back and look for our names. We cruised all around the islands. He said someday we'd explore Devil's Cave where a pirate hid from the British during the Revolution." She gave me another shake. "Are you listening, Robin?"

"I'm listening." My heart was shrinking up into a tight little ball.

"Chris is such a great guy. I never knew I could be comfortable with a boy. I think he likes me, and I can't wait for the rock concert next Saturday. Are you sure you didn't set him up to ask me? If I thought you did, I would never speak to you again!"

"Why would I do a thing like that?"

"You've tried it before. I can usually spot a setup

a mile away. I think Chris had a good time today. He's really fun to be with."

I know, I know, I thought. If I pretend I'm asleep maybe she'll go away.

"I still can't believe he asked me out. Do you know he's going to be a marine biologist?"

"Yes."

After a while she went to her room, but I lay awake for a long time.

I started work in the store on the Monday of Easter vacation, and Jeffrey spent most of the morning teaching me to make flower arrangements. In the bottom of a Delft blue container he placed a block of porous material to hold the stems of a spring flower display. Pink hyacinths, double narcissus, and miniature tulips made a charming display.

"Now you try one," Jeffrey said. "Take your pick of any flowers in the greenhouses."

I chose a white kitten container, and I felt all thumbs as I arranged pink and white daisies, flowering dogwood, and snapdragons.

"Super! My dad was right, Robin. You do have a nice touch with flowers."

He showed me tricks of the trade, like using florist's wire to strengthen stems, how to shape flower petals, and how to prevent leaves from curling by spraying the underside with clear plastic. "We start making our Christmas wreaths late in October and you can go all-out with your creativity."

"Creativity is not my strong point."

"We'll take a chance." He leaned on the counter.

"Robin, I put the *Algonquin* in the water today, and I'm planning on making a trial run this afternoon after work. I'd like you to come along."

Why not, I thought? Chris doesn't like me anymore. It won't hurt to be friends with Jeffrey as long as I kept our relationship casual. I wouldn't get involved seriously with a boy again for a long time. It was too painful.

"Sure. Anyone else going along?"

"Just you and me."

"I'll be your first mate."

"I'll see you at five o'clock. The *Algonquin* is down at the dock."

"How long will we be gone?" I asked.

"Two or three hours, if the boat doesn't take on water or the motor doesn't conk out."

"I'll call my mother and tell her not to expect me for supper."

"We can catch something to eat at one of the waterfront restaurants."

Working with flowers all afternoon gave me time to sort out my thoughts and evaluate all the things that were happening to me. Trying to be my own person and to show responsibility toward my job had cost me Chris. Was it worth it? I knew I could never relinquish my independence, never abondon the right to control my life. Was this empty, aching feeling inside me part of the price? I had read somewhere that to accept love is to invite pain. It didn't seem fair.

At five o'clock I washed up, brushed my hair, braided it with a bright scarf, and joined Jeffrey down on the dock where the *Algonquin* was ready to cast off, its mahogany wood gleaming in the afternoon sun. Shoals of panfish flashed through the blue-green water in the shadow of the boat, and the sea gulls dived at us with their harsh little cries.

I climbed on board and settled back in the red leather seat. "If you need me, just whistle, captain."

"I'll let you off easy today." Jeffrey was at the wheel as we moved out in the river, standing with his strong, muscular legs slightly apart and wearing cutoff jeans. He was bare to the waist and bronzed from the long hours in the sun in the greenhouses. He was everything a girl could want in a boy—handsome, competent, intelligent. But why was I comparing him with Chris?

The *Algonquin* purred along smoothly, and Jeffrey was practically bursting with pride. "Listen to that motor! It makes all the hours I spent on it worthwhile."

I went up front and sat beside him. "Jeffrey, this trial run is very important to you. Why did you ask me to come along? Why not Stephanie or some of your other friends?"

He turned and looked at me. "Robin, haven't you been getting any vibes? Can't you tell I like you?"

Oh, no, I thought. I sat hugging my knees.

"I won't pretend I haven't heard the stories going around school. I know you and Chris broke up."

"I just want to be friends, Jeffrey. I hope you understand."

"It's none of my business, but what happened between you and Chris?"

"A clash of personalities."

"Some of the rumors say he dropped you for your sister. I can't buy that."

"They could be right."

"I'm more inclined to think you dropped him. I even had the crazy notion you dropped him for me."

"Wrong guess. I don't want to get involved with anyone for a long time."

"You must be hurting."

I didn't answer. I watched the white spray flying as a water skier in the distance cut the water. I didn't like to discuss personal problems. My mother always said I held my worries close to me like a child clutching a doll.

"I got off to a bad start with you, Robin, but I explained how it happened."

"That's ancient history now—I don't hold grudges. I just need time to think things out," I said.

"I don't give up easily. I want a chance to show you I'm not the jerk I appeared to be."

"Okay. We'll be friends."

He smiled. "Friendships can catch fire and take off."

"You'd make a great salesman, Jeffrey."

About ten miles up the river Jeffrey pulled up at the pier of a waterfront restaurant called The Sandpiper. "Can we go in like this?" I asked.

"They're used to people coming in off their boats. We'll eat in the lounge. No ties or suit coats are required there, but for convention's sake I'll pull on a jersey. The sight of my hairy, manly chest might rattle the waitresses."

"Come on, Jeffrey, I don't see more than half a dozen hairs."

Even the lounge was rather elegant, and I felt disheveled and ill-at-ease in the clothes I'd worked in all day. Thankfully, the interior was quite dark, with candles at each table and old-fashioned gaslights on the walls. We sat down in a curved booth upholstered in red velvet, and the waiter brought us sixteen-inch menus with red-flocked covers.

"Couldn't we have gone to McDonald's?" I said in a stage whisper.

"Relax. They probably think we're from one of the homes on Millionaire Row."

"I doubt it."

We ordered prime ribs of beef, and the waiter wheeled up a service cart with salad greens, cruets of oil and vinegar, mushrooms, tomatoes, and every other salad ingredient you could imagine. "Are you trying to impress me, Jeffrey?" I said after we made our salads and the waiter had left.

"I could be. I hope you're planning to come and see *Fiddler on the Roof*. We'll be winding up rehearsals after vacation."

"Rae sold my mother and me a pair of tickets. We'll be there."

"Rae is showing a lot of interest in the production. She and Mariann did a great job on the scenery, and now they're helping with the costumes," Jeffrey said.

"Attending a smaller school has done a lot for my sister. She was lost in a big city high school, but here she's making friends and joining in activities."

"That's good. Maybe we can get her to try out for some of our plays next year. How about you?"

140

"I have no stage ambitions. I'll usher or help print the programs. Will you be directing?"

"I hope so. I need all the experience I can get."

When we finished dinner and went out to the pier, we found a group of five or six people admiring the *Algonquin*. I could see Jeffrey's pride as he answered their questions.

As we started for home he said, "If it was warm we could go swimming. I know of a private beach nearby. I want to teach you to scuba-dive this summer."

"You want to teach a native Californian to scuba-dive? I was diving with my father when I was ten."

"Sorry, I goofed on that one."

"I'll let you take me fishing this summer. Would you believe it, I've never fished."

"For a real thrill, I'll take you muskellunge fishing. They average fifteen to twenty-five pounds."

"It's a deal!"

After Easter vacation I only worked Saturdays at the store. Everything was geared now toward Memorial Day, and thousands of pots of geraniums were being grown to decorate the graves of servicemen. Gardeners were buying vegetable plants; porch boxes and rock gardens were being readied for summer blossoming.

Jeffrey was busy every afternoon after school with rehearsals, but we had a few dates. We went to the movies and played racquetball, and one Sunday we went hiking in the state park. I kept stressing a "friends only" relationship. "Love is a friendship that has caught fire," he kept reminding me.

After the rock concert Rae and Chris were considered a pair, and they began getting invitations to parties. When the phone rang these days it was often for Rae, and it wasn't always girl friends. She carried on long conversations with a boy in her art classes.

When I read old-fashioned novels I used to snicker when they referred to a young girl "blossoming out." Well, that seemed to describe Rae. She seemed prettier, if that was possible, and high-spirited. She started experimenting with hairstyles and makeup and took more interest in her clothes.

When I saw her at school with Chris, she looked so happy. That's what I had always wanted for her, but why did it have to be with Chris?

One morning as I was dressing for school, she poked her head in the door of my bedroom. "What should I wear? The smoky rose eyeshadow or the blue?"

"The smoky rose complements your hair."

"Do you think I'm applying my blusher too far back on my cheekbones?"

"No, it looks all right."

She came in my room and stared in the mirror. "Robin, do you still like Chris?"

"I never said I didn't like him."

"You know what I mean."

"Am I sobbing in my pillow? No."

"Don't forget the play is tomorrow night. Jeffrey asked me to help the cast with their makeup, so I won't be able to sit with you and mother. Why don't you come backstage after it's over?"

I nodded yes, and Rae went back to her room.

Fiddler on the Roof was scheduled to run three nights, and Mother and I attended the first performance. The musical, based on century-old traditions of Eastern Europe, is superb. I'd seen it in Los Angeles with my parents, but I enjoyed this production even more because I knew some of the players. Todd—Mariann's brother—played the part of Tevye, the father, and nearly brought down the house. I knew I'd be humming "If I Were a Rich Man" and "Matchmaker, Matchmaker" for days. Tiffany, as Yenta, got applause every time she appeared.

Afterward, Mother and I went backstage to compliment Jeffrey and the cast. Everyone was in high spirits over the success of the play. Rae came up to us, her cheeks flushed with excitement, "There's a party tonight for the cast and the stage crew. I'm going to stay."

"What time do you want me to pick you up?" my mother asked.

"Someone can bring me home. Probably Todd or Jeffrey."

Todd or Jeffrey. Rae was branching out. We were starting to leave when Chris came in the door. "Hi, I hear there's a party tonight," he said to Rae.

"It's just for the cast and crew, Chris."

"No guests?"

"I empathize, but it's just for those who worked on the production." She seemed eager to get back to her friends.

Chris looked embarrassed. "Sorry I asked. Do you need a ride home?"

"I'll find a ride. Don't worry about me," she answered.

Chris turned abruptly and left.

CHAPTER THIRTEEN

Mariann's brother Todd was graduating from high school, and his parents planned a party for the Sunday before graduation. Rae and I both received invitations. I didn't know Todd too well, but Rae had visited frequently at the Reynolds's home.

Sunday dawned a beautiful day, perfect for a lawn party. "What shall I wear?" I asked Rae. Jeff had several graduation parties to attend and had told me he'd drop in later.

"I think I'll wear a dress," she answered. "I feel like dressing up. Maybe the yellow print I bought before we left California. I've only worn it once."

"I could wear my pleated skirt and white blazer. Suppose everyone is in jeans?"

"So what? We'll be different."

"What are you giving Todd?"

"A gift certificate from Barnard's. I'll put your name on it, too. You don't know him very well so there's no reason for you to give a separate gift," Rae said.

"After all, I'm a guest. I could put some money in a card."

"Don't worry about it."

"What's Mariann doing this summer?"

"She has a job as lifeguard at the state park. Todd will be working at the wildlife preserve. He's going to Clarkson in the fall."

"Can I ride with you and Chris?"

"I'm not going to the party with Chris."

I tried to sound casual. "How come?"

She shrugged. "I'm teaching him a lesson. I wanted him to take me to the opening of a new art gallery in Watertown, but he said it would bore him to death."

"Are you sure you know what you're doing, Rae?"

"There are other boys I'm sure would take me. Alan Logan and I share a mutual interest in art. I could even ask Jeffrey."

"Jeffrey?"

"We got acquainted when he was directing the play and I was working on the scenery."

She took me by surprise. Rae knew I was dating Jeffrey occasionally.

"Come on." She laughed. "You said yourself you weren't serious about him."

I hesitated. "No, there's nothing serious between us."

"Then don't look so dumbfounded. Will you blow-dry my hair for me? It always looks better when you do it."

My mother said we could use her car to drive to the party. Cars and motorcycles lined both sides of the road as we approached the Reynolds's home. A built-in swimming pool sparkled in the sunlight. Dozens of kids milled about sampling refreshments from the picnic tables, and other couples were dancing on the patio to music from the stereo. Sedate little groups of relatives sat in the shade under the trees, visiting and commenting on Todd's guests.

We found a place to park near the tennis courts and walked toward the house. Loud talk and laughter came from the garage. Mariann hurried up to meet us. "Hi, I'm glad you came. I need someone to talk to. Some of the fellows brought six-packs and my folks don't like it. I'm afraid they'll say something to them and the kids will all leave."

"I don't think they'll leave with all this good food around. Look at the guys shoveling it in at the table."

"Just a few of the fellows are drinking, but they could spoil the party."

"Maybe they'll move on to another party."

"I hope you're right. I know of at least six parties today. Rae, would you help me bring out some more refreshments?"

I was left alone and I felt self-conscious. I should have offered to help Mariann. Everyone was paired off or in little groups, most of them seniors, and I knew so few kids in the senior class. Even the tree-tops leaned together with soft whispers in the wind. Jeff drove by the house with a carful of boys looking for a place to park. I wondered if he'd join the group partying in the garage.

Then I saw Chris talking to Dave and Cory, and my heart gave a wild thump. Our eyes met and he raised his hand in greeting. A wave of feeling swept over me. I missed him so.

"Robin," Cory called. "Come over here."

I felt awkward and a little embarrassed as I joined them. "This is our third party today, and I can't face another potato salad," Cory said.

"Are you having a party, Dave?" I asked, to make conversation.

"My folks gave a dinner party last night. Mostly relatives. Very boring."

"Dave was smart," Chris remarked. "He invited all his rich uncles and really cleaned up. That's what I'm going to do next year."

"My folks can take the money they'd spend on a party and send me on a cruise—the north coast of Spain, or Paris."

"Dream on!" Chris laughed.

"Dave, there's Jill. Excuse us a minute," Cory said. "I've got to get Jill's address. She's going to Cape Cod this summer."

Darn Cory. She had left Chris and me alone on purpose. He was wearing a blue knit shirt, as blue as his eyes, and he was so tanned his hair seemed blonder by contrast.

"What are your plans for the summer, Robin?"

"I'll be working full-time in the store."

"That's what you wanted, isn't it?"

"Yes, I can use the money." I was so aware of Chris. I felt almost hypnotized by his nearness, the sound of his voice. A silence followed. We had always had so much to talk about and now there was nothing.

We heard shouts from the garage and Todd came running out, pursued by three boys. He headed toward the tennis courts, but they caught him and dragged him back toward the pool. He was fighting every inch of the way.

"What are they doing?"

Chris was laughing. "They're going to throw him in the pool."

"But he's dressed up!"

"Let's hope everything is wash-and-wear!" As I watched, the boys heaved Todd into the pool. I expected him to be furious but he came to the surface laughing, grabbed a ladder, and pulled himself up. The boys scattered as he took off after them.

Then someone pushed Dave in the pool. Pandemonium broke loose as other kids were tossed in. The party was getting rough! The girls didn't escape, either. I heard Cory shrieking as she was thrown in. Everyone was laughing and screaming. Chris left to join the fun.

I had no intention of getting tossed in the pool wearing my new blazer. The label said "Dry clean only." I didn't want my new sandals soaked either, or they would warp out of shape.

I ran toward the house to find a place to hide. I wanted to warn Rae and Mariann, too, to stay in the house if they didn't want to get thrown in. Rae couldn't swim and she'd be terrified if she was tossed in. I went through the house looking for them. They must have gone outside again.

I decided to hide in the den until things quieted down. From the safety of the window I watched the commotion outside. I hoped no one would start a fight—that would surely ruin the party.

"You're next, Robin! You can't hide in here!" Jeffrey came striding toward me.

"Jeffrey! No! Don't throw me in!" I begged.

He put his arm around me. "I wouldn't be so mean," he said softly. His face was close to mine.

"They're ruining the party!"

"The host always gets tossed in the pool at graduation parties around here—if there is a pool."

"If that's a tradition, I think it's terrible! Do they have to include the guests?"

"Some of them were practically begging to get thrown in. It's a sign of belonging if you walk around in wet clothes."

"I don't think the beer helped, either."

"It's just a party, Robin." He drew me close and his lips brushed my hair. "I've been on probation long enough. Haven't you learned to like me just a little?"

"I like you, Jeffrey." I felt uncomfortable.

"Then it's time you showed me." He gave me a long, lingering kiss.

I stirred in his arms. "Jeffrey . . ." He kissed me again, a more demanding kiss.

I heard a sound and saw Rae standing in the doorway, her face mirroring astonishment and disbelief. She gave a sob, then turned and ran from the room.

Jeffrey released me. "Who was that?"

"It was Rae. I've got to find her."

He was annoyed. "Why?"

"She's upset."

"What has she got to be upset about?"

"I think she likes you."

"Rae? We're friends but—"

"I have to go, Jeffrey." I hurried from the room. Outside the crowd had quieted down. The exertion must have given the guys a renewed appetite, for they were crowded around the refreshment table again. Some of the girls had gone home to change their clothes.

I saw Chris and I hurried over to him. "Have you seen Rae?"

"Yes, she ran past me and started down the road."

"She can't walk home. It's nearly two miles!"

"I think that's what she's doing."

"I'll get the car."

Chris caught my arm. "Robin, when are you going to stop being your sister's keeper? Rae is tougher than you give her credit for—she's perfectly capable of taking care of herself."

"You don't understand."

"Oh, yes I do. I've come to know Rae very well and she's a self-serving person. I also know what a pushover you are for her. Why don't you start thinking about yourself?"

I turned away but he wouldn't let me go. "Robin, I still care for you. Can't we try once more?"

"Why? Because you and Rae are having trouble?"

"It's always been you, Robin. Any other girl is just a poor imitation of you."

I wanted to believe him but I felt so mixed-up. "I have to go, Chris."

I found my car and started down the road. I saw

Rae far ahead, a little figure in a yellow dress. I pulled up alongside her. "Rae, get in! What's the matter with you?"

She turned on me, her eyes bright with accusation. "You're a sneak! You think you can take any boy away from me because I'm handicapped! You're making a big play for Jeffrey now just because you think I like him!"

I just stared at Rae, too startled to speak.

"I saw you talking to Chris behind my back! All your life you always got any boy you wanted and I had to sit back and watch you. Now you're trying to get Chris back, too."

Something stirred within me. I felt my anger rising and I faced my sister as an equal, not someone to be pampered and protected. "Don't blame me if it didn't work out for Chris and you! I'm sick of your using your handicap to avoid facing reality. It had nothing to do with any trouble you and Chris might have had!"

She glared at me. "Don't try to cover up!"

"Do you think handicapped people are the only ones who get hurt? Not by a long shot! I've been hurting ever since Chris and I broke up."

"A lot you understand!"

"We all have handicaps and they don't have to be physical. We just have to make the most of what we do have."

"Did you read that in a self-help book?"

I ignored her remark. "Chris told me he still likes me and I believe him. You have to take the same chances I do. If you want a steady boyfriend you have to risk rejection. I'm going to try to go back with Chris. You can do what you want."

We glared at each other like two contenders in a boxing ring. "Do you want to go back to the party or do you want to go home?" I asked.

"I will not go back to that party!"

"Then get in and I'll take you home."

"Don't think I'm going to ride with you!"

"If you don't get in, I'll go back and get one of the boys to *put* you in!"

Rae gave me an ugly look but she climbed in the car and slammed the door. We drove home in silence. I was so shook up over my outburst I was trembling.

The next few days were terrible. Rae refused to speak to me. We passed each other in the house like strangers. At first my anger had felt good, like a dip in a mountain stream, but now doubt settled over me. Had I driven Rae back into her shell again? Should I apologize? Thankfully, my mother was busy with her new job and didn't notice the strained atmosphere in the house.

Wednesday evening I was cleaning my room when Rae came in unexpectedly and sat down on my bed. "I thought you'd like to know I'm accepting Dad's offer to spend the summer with him."

"You're going alone?"

"Yes. I called him this afternoon and told him to expect me on the twenty-sixth. He'll make the arrangements for me to start classes July fifth."

"That's wonderful, Rae! You've never traveled alone."

"I can handle it. Isn't it about time?" She paused. "I didn't mean all those things I said on Sunday."

"I guess things did get out of hand."

"I don't want to be with Chris anymore, but he gave me confidence in myself. I'll always be grateful for that." She smoothed down her skirt. "We had good times together, but we weren't really right for each other. He kept talking about you and I was getting interested in other boys." She stood up. "I'm looking forward to a great summer in Chicago."

When Rae had left I sat for a long time without moving. I didn't know what the future held for Chris and me. His jealousy and my need for independence might continue to cause problems, but I hoped we could work them out. I was sure of one thing. I was going to begin to shake off the feelings of guilt that had plagued me all my life because of Rae's handicap. Chris was right. Rae was tougher than I had given her credit for.

I was free to go my own way, secure in the knowledge that my sister could cope with her own problems. I looked forward with enthusiasm to the summer vacation and my senior year ahead.

I stood up and stretched. It was good to feel free!